DREAM WITH ME

A WITH ME IN SEATTLE NOVEL

KRISTEN PROBY

AMPERSAND PUBLISHING, INC.

Dream With Me
A With Me In Seattle Novel
By
Kristen Proby

Dream With Me

A With Me In Seattle Novel

By Kristen Proby

Copyright © 2020 by Kristen Proby

All Rights Reserved. This book may not be reproduced, scanned, or distributed in any printed or electronic form without permission from the author. Please do not participate in or encourage piracy of copyrighted materials in violation of the author's rights. All characters and storylines are the property of the author and your support and respect is appreciated. The characters and events portrayed in this book are fictitious. Any similarity to real persons, living or dead, is coincidental and not intended by the author.

ISBN: 978-1-63350-056-3

Cover Photo by: JW Photography

Cover Design by: Hang Le

Published by Ampersand Publishing, Inc.

This one is for John, who encourages me to chase my dreams every day.

CHAPTER ONE

~ANASTASIA~

"*T*his isn't going to work."

I blow out a breath and stare at the shit-tastic mess I've scribbled on my sketchpad in disgust.

The idiots who hired me, and no, I don't always refer to my clients as idiots, didn't give me a place to start. When a couple wants a wedding cake, they usually come to me with photos they've pinned on Pinterest or found in magazines. They have colors and flowers they prefer.

They have a bloody vision.

But the people who marched into my bakery a month ago? They had none of that.

"We want you to go with your own vision," they said with wide-eyed smiles and imaginary cartoon hearts bursting over their heads. *"You're an artist, and we wouldn't dream of intruding on your process."*

I appreciate their vote of confidence. I really do.

And, sometimes, clients are *too* stringent in what they want.

"*I want* exactly *this*," some brides will say, and I have to gently remind them that I don't copy others' work.

But at least tell me what colors your flowers are. Throw me a damn bone!

It's not *my* wedding.

I've been in the wedding cake biz for a dozen years, and while living in California, I was lucky enough to be on *Best Bites TV*, designing and executing massive works of sugar that would make the most discerning art critics weep with joy.

But now I live near my hometown of Seattle, Washington, where my family is, and I've opened a new business here. I love it. It fuels me and exhausts me, just as a person's passion should.

But today, there's nothing in my well of ideas. My muse has decided to go on vacation, and she didn't give me any warning.

Fucking muse.

When this happens, which isn't often, I find it's best to step away from my kitchen.

So, I pack up my sketchbook and pencils, get in the car, and get ready to battle Seattle traffic.

Once on the road, I call my sister, Amelia. She likes to go to museums with me, and sometimes, the conversation alone will get my mind churning with new ideas.

"Hello, favorite sister," she says when she answers.

"I'm headed over to the glass museum," I say immediately. "Wanna go?"

"I would *love* to, but I'm recording today, and I have to do three videos to catch up. I'm sorry."

Lia is a super successful YouTube sensation. She films makeup tutorials and reviews products. With more than three million followers and her own makeup brand in the works, I couldn't be prouder of her.

Not to mention, she has a new husband who keeps her more than busy.

"I get it. I miss you, though. I haven't seen you in weeks. So, let's try to do a girls' night out, okay?"

"Yes, please. I'm down for that."

"Soon. Like, tomorrow night."

"Hold please." She pulls the phone away from her mouth but doesn't bother to cover it, so I can hear everything. "Wyatt? Babe, Stasia's on the phone and wants to do girls' night tomorrow night. Do we have plans? Oh, right."

I tap my fingers on the steering wheel, surprised that traffic through downtown is as light as it is.

"Hey, sorry, I can't tomorrow night. We're supposed to go to a gala for the new cardiothoracic wing at the hospital. Jace asked us weeks ago."

Our family is big and a little confusing. A diagram and a Ph.D. in astrophysics might be necessary to figure out who belongs to whom, and how we all fit together.

Wyatt is Amelia's husband. His brother, Jace, is the chief of staff in cardiothoracic surgery at Seattle General. Jace is a big deal. Actually, there's a lot of that in our family.

"We'll find a night to get together," I reply.

"Actually, you should come with us," Lia says, excitement in her voice. "I have dresses you can choose from and borrow, and I'll totally do your hair and makeup. It'll be fun. Say yes. Say it right now."

"Like my ass will fit in any of your dresses. Besides, I have *so much* work, Lia. I can't waste a whole day on a gala where I won't know anyone."

"You'll know me and Wyatt. And Jace and Joy. Levi and Starla will be there, too."

I sigh because, deep down, I want to go. I don't get to dress up often, and I love hanging out with Wyatt's brothers and their wives. Not to mention, I never get to see my sister.

But I have a wedding cake due on Saturday morning that's only half-decorated, and I really have to get this other cake designed so I can get to work on it first thing on Sunday.

"You're too quiet. You're thinking of a way you can ditch work so you can go, so just *do it*."

I bite my lip. If I stay up all night tonight finishing Saturday's cake, I can make it work.

"Okay. I'll go."

"Yay," Lia says with a little squeak, making me

laugh. "Be at my house by noon so we can start getting ready."

"What time is the gala?"

"Eight," she says.

"It will not take eight hours to get ready."

"You're going to look like a goddess when I'm through with you," Lia promises. "See you tomorrow!"

She hangs up, and I wrinkle my nose. The guilt of taking time away from work that I don't have settles between my shoulder blades.

But one of the things I've been working on this year is taking more time for *me*. I moved out of California because it was killing me. I was working fifteen-hour days, seven days a week, and the result of that was illness and despair. I've battled asthma all my life, and the long hours and some of the spices in the bakery were hell on me. Now, I have my own shop where I can control the environment, along with how many hours a day I work, and I can admit, my asthma has been better. Taking care of myself is important.

And taking one day to be with my family is part of that self-care.

Working through the night is totally worth it.

THIS WAS THE RIGHT CALL. Being out of the bakery today and immersed in art is exactly what I needed for a fresh perspective. Soaking in someone else's vision always renews my passion for my own creativity.

It seems my muse likes to hang out in museums.

And the O'Callaghan Museum of Glass in Seattle is my very favorite of all of them.

I'm sitting on a bench in the middle of one of the exhibit rooms, soaking it all in.

I've never met Kane O'Callaghan, the artist who creates such beauty. He seems to love color, as it's splashed around me. In this room, the glass is shaped like water, waves crashing on beaches with marine life floating around. Blues, greens, and white with splashes of yellow and red here and there tickle my senses.

I can practically hear the beach around me.

With the hair standing on my skin, I reach for my sketchpad and pencils. With my legs crossed, I get to work, my pad in my lap.

People walk past me, but I hardly notice them. I'm consumed by the design that's taking shape in my head and on the paper. I take breaks, looking up at the glass, the color, the fluidity of the work, and then keep sketching.

I don't know if I've ever drawn a full concept so quickly.

Once I'm finished, I take a deep breath and notice my chest is beginning to feel heavy. I glance around, surprised to see a man sitting on the bench opposite mine, watching me with lazy, green eyes.

"Can I help you?" I ask the handsome stranger. He

has dark hair with matching stubble on his chin, and eyelashes framing those bright green orbs.

"I was just going to ask you the same question," he says with a voice laced with milk chocolate.

"I'm just enjoying the exhibit," I say, giving him a polite smile.

"Looks like you're enjoying your little drawing there," he replies, nodding at the pad in my lap. I close it and drop the smile.

"Just working," I say.

"In a museum?"

I blow out a breath of impatience. "Do you work here?"

He tilts his head to the side, watching me. "Not really."

"Then it's none of your business, is it?"

"Are you one of those people who sits in museums and copies the art there because you can't come up with original work of your own?"

"Are you always an asshole, or just today?" I retort, getting more pissed by the second. "Surely, I'm not the only person in the world who gets inspired by art. In fact, I think that's the point of it."

He doesn't say anything, just blinks and watches me quietly. He's not creepy. I don't get a dangerous vibe from him. If I did, I'd run out of here and alert security.

"Can I see the sketch?" he asks, surprising me.

"It's just a—"

"I'd still like to see it." His lips tip up in a half-smile

that would melt far stronger women than I, and he holds his hand out, waiting for me to pass over my pad.

Finally, I flip through the pages to what I was just working on and pass it over to the handsome stranger.

His eyes narrow as he examines the crude drawing. I instantly wish I'd used more color and been more thorough, but it's only supposed to be for *my* eyes. A guideline for when I start decorating the cake in just a couple of days.

"There is no water here," he says in surprise and looks up at me. "It doesn't look anything like the glass in this room."

"Why would it?" I frown. "I'm *inspired*, not copying. Besides, that's just a sketch. When I make the final piece, I'll know what I was thinking when I thought it up."

"I see." He passes it back to me. "I like it very much. You've a good eye."

Is that a slight accent I hear in his voice? I take a deep breath, relieved that the heaviness is gone from my lungs. If I'm not mistaken, I can *smell* him. It's a lovely, woodsy scent that's light and masculine and, well…sexy.

"What are you doing here?" I ask.

He shrugs a shoulder and glances around the room. "Remembering, I suppose."

Before I can ask him what he means by that, a woman comes rushing into the room, her heels clicking on the hardwood floor.

"Kane, we need you in the storeroom. Now, when you see what happened, don't kill anyone."

"If a piece is broken, I can't guarantee that I won't commit murder." He glances back at me. "I guess our pleasant visit is over, then."

"Wait. Are you Kane O'Callaghan?"

"One and the same." He stands and holds out his hand to shake mine. "And you are?"

"Embarrassed," I mutter as I slide my hand into his. "I won't tell you I love your work. I guess that's clear enough."

"But an artist never tires of hearing it," he replies with a wink before nodding at the frazzled woman. "Have a good time. And take all the time you need."

With that, he hurries away, and I'm left in the amazing room, flustered.

I just met Kane O'Callaghan. I showed him my sketch. He was a bit gruff, borderline rude, and I managed to call him an asshole.

"Good one, Anastasia."

"THIS IS FUN," I mutter while Amelia tickles my cheekbone with a fluffy brush. "We don't do this often enough anymore."

"I know. And I get to do this for a *living*. You should be in one of my videos." Her blue eyes widen in excitement. "Seriously, I could do your makeup in the video and show different techniques for working on someone else. It's *so* different from applying my own makeup. It would be fun."

"Maybe one day."

Where Amelia is gorgeous with amazing cheekbones and a slender body, I'm different. We share the same blond hair and signature Montgomery blue eyes, but I'm curvier than she is, with wider hips and boobs.

I'm not exactly the kind of girl who models on fashion vlogs.

Don't get me wrong, I'm fine with how I look. I *like* my curves. And when I'm done up, well, I look pretty fly, but I'm no fashion model.

"We'll do it next month when the new eyeshadow palette releases," she says as if it's all settled. I just stay quiet. I'll do it for her. It seems I'll do just about anything for my siblings.

"Have you talked to Archer lately?" I ask her. Archer is the eldest, and our only brother.

"Yeah, I tried to get him to come with us tonight, but getting our brother in a suit is like talking a fish out of the water."

I laugh at the thought. "It's too bad because he's handsome when he's all dressed up."

"I'm just happy that I managed to get him in a suit for our wedding," Lia replies and stands back to check out her handiwork. "I think you're ready. Next up is the dress."

"Let me see."

"Not until you're dressed." She leads me through her massive master bedroom to the equally enormous closet. "I've chosen three that will look *so* amazing on you."

"I'll never fit into them," I remind her.

"They're A-line, and they'll show off your incredible legs," she says, waving me off. "Try the red one first."

I slip out of the silky robe she insisted I put on so I didn't have to pull a shirt over my head after my makeup was done, and pull the dress up my legs. It gets stuck on my thighs.

"Told you."

"Okay, this one." She passes me a black dress with sparkly fake diamonds scattered across the bodice. Once I wrangle it up over my hips, and she zips up the back, it fits me like a glove. I stare in the mirror, my hands smoothing down the light material. Amelia did a hell of a job on my makeup. But then again, she always does.

"My boobs look fantastic in this," I mutter, admiring the ample cleavage the dress shows off without making me look like I'm a stuffed sausage. The hemline ends just below my knees, and the material floats around my legs like a cloud. "Oh, and it's light and comfy."

"Perfect," Lia says with a bright smile. "It looks ah-mazing on you. You can totally keep it."

"You don't have to—"

"It's Versace."

"I'm totally keeping it."

Lia laughs and steps into her own pink dress that slips off her shoulders, making her look like a faerie princess. Once dressed, she stands next to me, and we admire ourselves in the mirror.

"We're hot, sweet sister of mine," she says. She leans in to kiss my cheek, but I pull away. Lia's always trying to cuddle me, kiss me, or hug me.

I secretly like it, but I can't tell her that.

"Hell, yes, we're hot."

Wyatt's waiting downstairs for us, dressed in a classic black tuxedo, and as soon as we reach him, we're off, headed for the gala. At this time of night, traffic is light, so we quickly reach the hotel where the shindig is being held.

We're helped out of the car, and once inside, I reach for a glass of champagne and look for our people.

"There's our table," Wyatt says, pointing to a round table where Levi and Jace are sitting, their heads together as they talk. "I'm going to join my brothers."

"We're going to mingle," Lia says and takes my hand in hers. "Let's find Joy and Starla. I bet they're by the food."

"I could use food."

Sure enough, Joy and Starla are at the appetizer buffet, loading up tiny plates with canapes and crab cakes.

"I'm so happy you guys are here," Joy says with a sigh. "I mean, I've been coming to these things with

Jace forever, but it's exhausting to try and make small talk when you don't know anyone, you know?"

"We've got you," Starla says. The pop star is dressed in a killer strapless green dress that has a slit up the side to her hip. Red-soled heels are the perfect touch. She turns to me, a wide smile on her face. "Wow, girl, you clean up nice."

"It was all Amelia's doing. I can bake a cake like a champ, but I'm worthless when it comes to makeup."

"Good thing she has me," Amelia says with a wink.

While the other three chat about dresses and hairstyles, I glance around the room, not expecting to see anyone I know. I love my brother-in-law, but I don't walk in the same social circles as he does.

There's a glass sculpture in the middle of the room that I immediately recognize, and I wander away from the others to check it out.

Vivid red, orange, and yellow; twisty, swirling shapes that reach for the ceiling. I'd recognize the work anywhere.

This is an O'Callaghan piece.

I stand and sip my bubbly drink, examining the craftsmanship in the glass, then notice a discreet plaque that says it's part of the silent auction.

I'm positive that I can't afford it. His pieces go for thousands, sometimes *hundreds* of thousands of dollars.

My family is wealthy, but that's out of my price range.

But maybe, just maybe I can put in a bid.

I wander over to the silent auction bids and see that the sculpture is already well into the six figures and kiss that dream goodbye.

Someday, maybe, I'll own one of Kane's pieces.

I shrug a shoulder and turn to walk away, almost colliding with a broad chest.

"Oh, pardon me," I say. When my eyes travel up the strong chest and over the recently shaven square jawline, I look into mossy green eyes.

Kane O'Callaghan.

"We meet again," he says with a small smile.

"It seems we do." I take a deep breath, and the smell of someone's perfume fills my nostrils. My lungs immediately tighten. As much as I want to stay and talk with him, ask him a million questions, I have to get to a restroom.

I need my rescue inhaler.

Damn it!

I take two big steps and begin the mental speech to talk me down from a full-on panic attack.

You're fine. You're breathing fine. Slow breaths, Anastasia. It's just a little perfume, that's all.

I try to smile his way, and then turn away again. I guess if I have a full-on asthma attack here and now, there are roughly forty-seven doctors who can save the day.

I walk into the women's restroom and open my clutch, pull out my inhaler, and take a long pull off it, relieved when the albuterol fills my lungs. I immediately feel relief.

See? You're fine. All better. No reason to panic.

Let's not even consider the fact that this is the second time in two days that I've managed to make a fool of myself in front of Kane.

I stuff the inhaler back into my clutch and walk out of the restroom where Kane is leaning against the wall, his hands in his pockets, looking casual and calm as he watches me walk through the door.

"Was it something I said?" he asks.

"I'm sorry, I didn't mean to rush off."

"All better?" His lips turn up in that half-smile.

"Better." I nod, not wanting to get into my medical issues. "That piece you donated is stunning."

"Thank you." He slips a hand out of his pocket and reaches out for mine. "Dance with me."

"*Dance* with you?"

He quirks an eyebrow. "Please."

CHAPTER TWO

~ANASTASIA~

Okay, so the man has moves. It shouldn't surprise me that someone who creates such amazing works of art can also lead a girl around the dance floor. With one palm firmly planted on my lower back, and the other clutching my hand, Kane keeps his eyes on mine.

"You're a good dancer," I murmur.

"You're nervous," he replies softly. "There's no need to be. It's just a dance."

I take a deep breath and offer him a smile. He's right. It's just a dance.

The fact that he's maybe the hottest man I've ever seen is a huge bonus.

And if he can move like this, with all of our clothes *on*, I can only imagine what it could be like if we were naked.

Mercy.

"I never got your name," he says and guides me closer to him so we can talk into each other's ears. I glance around the room, seeing my sister and the other girls smiling at us, watching us dance.

"Anastasia," I say and turn my head, not quite planting my nose against his neck. The smell of this man is going to kill me.

And not because it triggers my asthma.

Because it's too sexy.

I watch the pulse in his neck and enjoy the feeling of his strong arms holding me.

"That's a lovely name." The accent is thicker in his voice now. Irish? I'm not good with accents, but I'd bet he's Irish.

His last name might be an indicator.

"Thank you."

The song ends and flows into another ballad. Adele sings about finding another lover, as Kane moves against me, with me.

I wonder if it looks as sexy as it feels.

"You said yesterday," he whispers against my ear, "that you'd be using your sketch for something else. What will that something be?"

"A cake."

He pulls back far enough to smile down at me in surprise. "A cake, is it?"

I nod, more comfortable talking about what I do for a living than just dancing in silence.

"I design and build wedding cakes for a living. I can

do them for other occasions, as well, but wedding cakes are what I'm known for."

"Interesting."

"I have a client who came into my shop about a month ago to hire me. They didn't give me any direction at all. No colors, no requests. It just has to feed about two hundred guests." I shake my head in disgust. "Not that I want them to tell me to copy a photo. I won't do that, but usually, they have colors they like or flowers in mind. *Something.* Not these two. When I need inspiration, I like to look at what others have created. Or have conversations with people I enjoy."

"That makes sense," he says and leans in to kiss my forehead, which sends a shiver right down my spine to my lady parts—which had already sat up and taken notice of Kane.

"What was that for?" I ask.

"An apology," he replies. "For being difficult yesterday."

"Apology accepted."

His lips quirk into that half-smile, his green eyes shining. The song is almost over, and I know I should thank him for the dance and find Lia and the others.

"Thanks for the dance."

The last note plays, and I pull back, immediately wishing I was back in his arms.

He's a stranger, and it's crazy, but it's true.

"Do you belong to a man, Anastasia?" Kane brushes his knuckles down the side of my cheek.

I frown. "I'll never *belong* to anyone."

"You know what I mean. Are you taken?"

"I'm single if that's what you're asking."

"Good." He kisses the back of my hand. "I have a room here for the night. Join me."

I blink at him. If I'm not mistaken, Kane O'Callaghan just invited me up to his hotel room. I'm not naïve. I know what he's proposing.

And every single brain cell in me screams, *this is not a good idea.*

But my body says, *hell yes, it's a great idea.*

"I'm here with people."

He nods. "Let's find them, then."

I laugh, a full-on guffaw because this is just so ridiculous. And because I'm totally going to do as he suggests.

That self-care thing I was talking about? Maybe it includes enjoying a random night with a hot stranger once in my life. It's not like this happens often. But once? What the hell.

I walk off the dance floor, not bothering to glance behind me to see if Kane's following me. He is. I can feel his eyes on me.

"Hey," Lia says with a huge smile. "And you didn't think you'd know anyone here."

"This is Kane O'Callaghan," I say, introducing Kane to our group. "Amelia is my sister."

"You're the spitting image of each other," Kane says, flashing a grin.

I make the rounds at the table, pointing out Jace and his brothers and their wives. When I get to Starla, Kane's eyes widen.

"I listen to your music in my barn," he says.

"And I have pieces of yours in my homes," she says with a smile. "It's a pleasure to meet you."

"I do believe the pleasure is mine." Kane's green eyes turn down to me. "Shall we say goodnight, then?"

"Wait, what?" Levi, one of the cops in our family says with narrowed eyes. "You just got here."

"If you don't mind, I'd like to have Anastasia to myself for a while," Kane says as he slips his hand into mine.

Lia stands and hugs me. "Call me later and tell me *everything*."

I wave at the table, ignoring Levi's overprotective stare, and let Kane lead me out of the convention room to the elevators.

"This is crazy," I whisper as we step into the cab. "Aren't you here with anyone?"

"My agent, Peter," Kane says. "He won't miss me. Donating the piece is for a good cause, and making a personal appearance sold a few extra tickets. But I showed up, and now I'd like to spend some time with the mysterious cake artist that I've managed to run into twice in two days."

"I'm really not that mysterious."

"You are to me," he says, and once the elevator

reaches the penthouse, he takes my hand and leads me into his *room.*

Which is way too generic of a word for what this is.

Kane's staying in the biggest suite the hotel has to offer. Not just a *room.*

He leads me into the living area that has floor-to-ceiling views of the lights of downtown Seattle.

"Would you like some wine? Or anything, for that matter? We can order room service if you'd like."

"A glass of wine is great." I sit on the couch and cross my legs, watching as Kane walks about the space, opens a wine fridge, and pulls out a bottle of white. He uncorks and pours and then passes me a glass.

He's a tall man, with long limbs and broad shoulders. His white shirt hugs his muscles when he takes off his jacket and rolls up his sleeves.

God, I love the way a man looks in a white shirt with rolled sleeves.

And then, when tattoos are revealed on one of his arms? I almost spit out my wine.

"Tell me more," he says as he sits across from me.

"I feel like I'm in a job interview."

He sips his drink, watching me. "I haven't any interest in hiring you for any job. I just want to get to know you."

"Why?"

He lifts an eyebrow. "Because I'm interested. And that means I want to know more. You're a beautiful woman, Anastasia."

"Thank you."

"How did you get into cake design?"

"I thought I wanted to be a chef." I grin at the memory and kick off my heels, pulling my feet up under me to get comfortable. "All my life, I told anyone who would listen that I'd be a famous chef someday. And then I went to culinary school, and I was *awful*."

"How so?"

"It just wasn't for me. I burned things, spilled things, you name it. Being clumsy when you're pulling a roast out of the oven isn't convenient."

I see laughter in his eyes as he nods. "I can see that."

"But then we had to do a rotation through the bakery, and I fell in love with it. Suddenly, I wasn't clumsy anymore. It was like my body just knew I was supposed to be there, and it all clicked. I enjoy working with sugar, the different mediums of it. My favorite is sugar sculpture, but it takes a lot of time and is expensive, so I don't do it often."

"Do you have photos of some of the cakes you've made?"

I blink at him, surprised. "Do you have a phone? You can Google me."

"I never carry a cell, and I've never Googled anything in my life," he replies.

"Are you a time traveler? This is 2020, Kane."

"All the phone does is interrupt my work, so I refuse to have it with me. It's probably dead in my kitchen right now."

I smile, charmed by him, and open my clutch to pull out my own phone. My inhaler falls out onto the floor and lands at Kane's feet.

He fetches it and passes it to me.

"Thanks."

He looks like he wants to ask questions, but before he can, I wake up my phone and bring up the album with my cakes. I gesture for him to sit next to me.

"You can just swipe left to look at the photos."

He settles near me, takes my phone, and looks at each photo intently, almost as if he's going to be quizzed on them later.

He comes to a cake I did last year. It has four tiers and is covered in magnolias.

"The flowers are pretty. Does the florist deliver them to you?"

"Those magnolias are sugar," I say softly, and smile when Kane's gaze whips to mine.

"They look real."

"Thank you. Each one took me two hours."

He looks back down at the phone. "How do I look closer?"

I pinch and spread my fingers on the image to magnify it for him.

"Incredible," he murmurs. "I'd love to see the tools you work with."

"Ditto."

He grins at me and then returns to the photos. Once he's seen all of them, he passes me the phone and waits while I put it to sleep and return it to my clutch.

"You're a talented woman, Anastasia."

"You can call me Stasia. Most people do."

He takes my hand and twines our fingers, then kisses my knuckles. "I prefer Anastasia."

"How did you get started with glass?"

"My uncle in Ireland blew glass and would let me sit in the barn with him when I was a lad. It was the most thrilling thing I'd ever seen, and I knew I wanted to do nothing else with the whole of my life."

"How long have you lived in the States?"

"Twenty years," he says, still touching me with strong, callused hands.

"Do you miss Ireland?"

"More than you'll ever know." He kisses my fingertips now. "I spend two months every year there, but the yearning never really goes away."

"Why don't you move back?"

He pauses, thinking it over. "My family's here, all near Seattle, and I love them too much to be gone from them."

I nod, completely understanding. "I get it. It's why I moved back here not long ago. My family's here. You met some of them tonight, which is kind of odd."

"Odd, is it?"

"A bit, yes. How many siblings do you have?"

"Four." He grins. "It's a large clan, the O'Callaghans."

"The Montgomerys are the same," I say with a wide

smile. It seems I have more in common with Kane than I expected. "Although I'm only one of three, we have more cousins than we can count, and they're all married with kids. We could be our own village."

"Montgomery," he murmurs. "'Tis a Scottish name, aye?"

"I do believe a great-grandfather came from Scotland, yes."

He stands and guides me to my feet.

"Are we headed to the bedroom?" I ask, "or are you kicking me out for being Scottish?"

"We'll get to the bedroom. And I think I can find it in my heart to forgive your heritage."

"You're a kind man."

"I'm not, no." He frowns. "I'd like to dance with you again."

"You like to dance, don't you?"

"I never have. Until tonight."

"You have a way with words," I inform him as he pulls me against him and wraps his long, strong arms around my waist, holding me close. He tips his head down and gently kisses my bare shoulder, sending shivers down my spine. I inhale sharply at my body's response to him, my hands tightening on his shoulders.

"Responsive." He kisses again. "Delicious. From the minute I saw you, sitting among my glass, I knew I'd eventually have you like this."

"I want that statement to make me mad," I admit,

but tip my head instead, giving him better access to my flesh.

"You shouldn't. You're a beautiful woman with passion in those gorgeous blue eyes of yours. Your irises are the same color as the glass in that room. I couldn't stop watching you, the intensity of how you attacked the sketch. It's how I feel when I'm working, and I've never seen it reflected in someone else before."

"I get lost in it," I admit, and feel my eyes drift closed when he drags his nose up to my ear. Good God, he's turned me into a puddle.

"Aye, as do I." His accent has intensified with lust and only pulls me deeper into his spell. We aren't moving to the music anymore. My hands knead his muscular shoulders, and Kane grips the pull of my zipper, then drags it down and lets my dress pool around my waist.

"It fits too tightly," I inform him with a grin. "I have to work it over my hips."

"Not yet," he says and lifts me into his arms as if I weigh nothing at all. He carries me to the bedroom where a sidelight is on next to the bed, the only illumination in the room. He sets me gently onto the duvet and watches me with those bright green eyes. "You're a vision, Anastasia."

"You're not so bad yourself." I bite my lip and reach out for him, silently inviting him to lie with me.

And he does.

But there's no frenzy, no tearing of clothes, no rush.

Instead, he cups my face and finally, *finally* brushes his full lips over mine, softly at first, and then he sinks into me, kissing me as if he's starved for me.

He knows his way around a woman's mouth, that's for sure. His lips nip, his tongue teases until I'm scissoring my legs, trying to relieve some of the pressure building between them.

Kane reaches for my hand and moves over me, hovering above me, planting my hand on the mattress by my head and kissing me for all he's worth.

"We're going to take our time," he promises.

I could be using the electric mixer, but that would mean that I couldn't mix by hand, and this is how I'm getting rid of my angry energy today.

I'm rage-baking.

This happens when I'm pissed at myself. Some people clean, others drink.

I bake.

And it's a good thing because I have a shit-ton to do in a small amount of time, and the rage-baking makes me move faster.

It works.

Of course, I'm also obsessing about last night, and that's *not* good.

Hence, the rage.

And the baking.

"Best sex of my damn life," I mutter, setting the hand mixer aside. I reach for a spatula and get to work scraping the dough off the sides of the bowl. "Of my *life*. And he's a stranger. I had sex with a stranger."

I blink rapidly, wondering what the hell I was thinking. Sure, Kane may be sexy and artsy and charming and kind of mysterious.

Did I mention sexy?

Because I had no idea. If I thought just the glimpse of ink on his arm was hot, it was the treat of the century when he got naked.

Naked Kane is fucking ridiculous.

And he knows what to do with a woman's body, bless him. Also? Don't even get me started on that accent. It's thicker when he's turned on, and he even said some words I didn't understand, which only made me wetter and want more.

But it was a one-night stand. And now that I know how good it is, I'm ruined for all time with any other man. Because no one will ever make my body hum the way Kane O'Callaghan did.

If I'm being honest, it's still humming.

Eight hours later.

I sigh, brush loose strands of hair off my cheek, and shriek when I turn around to find my brother, Archer, standing behind me.

"I knocked," he says, his hands up in surrender.

"I didn't hear it."

"I know. You were too busy muttering things about

sex to yourself. Yes, Lia called me, and no, I don't want details."

"That means the whole family knows."

"They do." He sidles up to my pile of scrap cake and shoves a big piece into his mouth.

"That's not for you."

"They're scraps," he says with his mouth full, spraying pieces of chocolate cake on my countertop.

"That's not sanitary."

"Pretty sure not much of what you did last night is sanitary. But again, I don't want to know."

"Why are you *here*?"

Archer grins. "Because I love you."

"You love my scraps."

He chomps happily. Keeping Archer and our cousin, Will, full is an ongoing battle. The two of them eat constantly.

"Wanna talk about him?" Archer asks.

"No. There's nothing to talk about. It was a one-time thing."

His face doesn't change, but I know this isn't what my overprotective brother wants to hear.

"Did he say that?"

"It was totally implied—and expected—from the beginning." I pour the batter into a round pan and slide it into the oven. "I left in the middle of the night."

"So, no goodbye? Or was he awake when you left?"

"He was asleep." I frown. "I couldn't sleep, and I didn't want an awkward goodbye this morning, so I slunk out and did the walk of shame through the lobby."

"You're a grown woman who can decide who she chooses to spend her time with. No shame in that."

I love my big brother. Archer is protective, but he's not a caveman about it. If I told him that Kane hurt me, which he did *not*, Archer would kick his ass.

But if I just want to talk without being judged, Archer will do that, too.

"You're right. And I had a good time."

"Then why were you muttering and trying to kill the mixing bowl when I walked in?"

I shrug a shoulder and brush my hair out of my eyes again. "Because I feel ridiculous."

"Well, you should. This scrap pile is puny, and I'm hungry."

"If I feed you cake all day, that will be my rent money for the month."

"I don't ask you to pay me rent, so whatever."

I laugh and pull a whole cake out of the fridge. The client changed their mind on the flavor of their cake at the last minute, so I have an extra.

I slide it over to Archer with a fork and watch as his stupidly handsome face breaks out into a wide grin.

"For me?"

"For you. Don't make yourself sick. Also? You're going to get fat if you keep eating all of this cake."

"Worth it," he says and shoves a big bite into his mouth. "Will you still love me if I have a big belly?"

I laugh and take a bite for myself. It's pretty good. Not dry. And the frosting is *so good.* I found the perfect recipe for buttercream.

I could eat it by the bucketful.

"So, no future with Mr. Glassman?"

"Uh, no." I toss my plastic fork into the trash and reach for a clean bowl. "He's a famous artist, and he found me interesting for five minutes. And I'm busy with cakes. Not to mention, he lives in Ireland part of the year."

"How horrible. Yes, he's awful. I can see why you bailed."

"You're a pain in my ass."

He smiles, cake in his teeth, and makes me laugh again. "That's what brothers are for, remember? Oh, Mom and Dad want to have dinner next weekend. The whole family's going to be there."

"The *whole* family?"

"Well, the ones who are in town, anyway. We're meeting at Uncle Steven and Aunt Gail's house next Sunday at two."

"Dinner at two?"

"It's a BBQ." He shrugs. "I'm just the messenger. Be there at two next Sunday."

"Okay. What are you doing today?"

"Isn't it obvious? I'm hanging out with you."

"Lucky me."

CHAPTER THREE

~KANE~

"Feckin hell." Sweat pours off me, soaking through the rag I have tied around my forehead and running down my face and my back.

That's not what's bothering me, though. When you work in a hot barn turning glass, you're going to sweat.

But I just broke the piece I'd been working on for two bleeding hours.

I toss my pipe onto a nearby table and rip the rag off my head with a snarl, reaching for my water bottle.

Murphy, my yellow Labrador, lifts his head, watching me warily.

"You've been no help today."

Murphy lowers his head to his paws and huffs out a long breath.

Knowing that I won't get any more work in this morning, I shut down the furnace and scowl as I walk to the sink to wash my hands, then shut the barn door behind us as Murphy and I walk toward the house.

I bought this property a dozen years ago after the museum was built in Seattle. My home, with my barn and trees, with its cliffs and views of the Pacific Ocean, is a good hour away from the city. If it hadn't been a pain in my ass, I would have moved even farther away from all of the people and the noise, but I didn't want to be too far from family.

If any of them ever needs me, I have to be able to get to them. And, truth be told, my door is always open to them, as well. It's many a night that an O'Callaghan comes out to my property to spend a day soul-searching, watching the water, and spoiling Murphy.

"Someone's here now," I murmur to the dog, who's stayed by my side during the walk between buildings. "Who is it, boy?"

Of course, I know the answer. My youngest sister, Mary Margaret, comes out to see me whenever her piece-of-shite husband is out of town on business.

I watch with narrowed eyes as she opens the boot—or trunk as the Americans call it—of her car and pulls out her case of belongings.

"Looks like Maggie will be with us for a few days."

Murphy barks, his whole body vibrating with excitement to go and greet one of his favorite people. But he's a good boy and waits for my command.

"Off you go, then."

That's all it takes for Murphy to take off like a shot,

barking with excitement. Maggie stops and looks our way, her face brightening into a smile as Murphy joins her, wagging his tail and soaking up lots of pats and kisses.

"Is the lemon out of town, then?" I ask as I approach, not at all worried when she scowls at me.

"You know I hate it when you call him that."

Maggie's husband is Joey Lemon, and we siblings find the name appropriate. Joey *is* a lemon, at least in the husband department.

Not that my sister will admit that. Not on this day or any other, for that matter. She married him young, just out of high school, and remains as faithful as the day she said her vows.

I simply raise a brow as I take the handle of her case and lead her into the house.

"Yeah, he's out of town for the rest of the week. He has a conference in Dallas."

I wonder what her name is.

I've suspected for years that the *conferences* aren't that at all, but rather an excuse for Joey to leave town with the flavor of the month.

I could easily hire an investigator to see if my suspicions are true, but it would hurt my sister, and I wouldn't do that for anything in the world.

"Your room's ready for you," I inform her as I walk to the back of the house to the room Maggie chose when I first bought the home and set her case by the king-sized bed. "You're welcome to stay for as long as you like."

"Just a few days," she murmurs, petting Murphy's head. "You would have known I was coming, but you never answer your damn phone."

"No need." I shrug and walk past her to the kitchen, then pull a bottle of water out of the fridge. "You still came all the same, didn't you?"

"But you would have had a heads-up," she says, shaking her head. We have the same argument weekly. "What if there's an emergency?"

"There are police on this island," I reply, the way I always do. "And they will come fetch me if need be."

She sighs and sits at the table, giving Murphy the perfect opportunity to lay his head in her lap.

I watch her and feel everything in me coil in rage when I see the bruise on her jawline.

"He put his fucking hands on you."

Her gaze whips up to mine, and she immediately shakes her head.

"No, I was trying to open something, and it was stuck. When it came free, I whacked myself in the chin. Joey's a lot of things, but he's never hit me, Kane. Honest."

I sip my water, seething. Yes, Joey *is* a lot of things.

"I wouldn't lie to you," she continues. "Also, you look angrier than normal this morning."

"I'm rarely angry."

"Moody then. You're always moody. What's wrong with you?"

I don't know that I'm comfortable telling my sister about the woman I had in my bed just three nights ago, or that the blasted woman left that bed while I slept.

"I've been working for three days."

"Straight?"

I shrug a shoulder and finish off my water, then toss the reusable bottle into the sink.

"I hate it when you do this," she says. "It's dangerous work when you've slept well, but to work for days on end without rest isn't safe at all, Kane."

"I love you, too." I kiss her head and walk out to the sunporch. I had it all glassed in so I could use it year-round and enjoy the view.

"That's not all that's bothering you."

"Have I ever told you that you're a pain in my backside, Mary Margaret?"

She tips her head to the side, watching me with eyes as green as the hills of Ireland. Both Maggie and our sister, Maeve, have deep auburn hair, while the men in the family—me, Keegan, and Shawn—were blessed with dark hair.

Two gingers in the family are quite enough. Their tempers are unparalleled.

"It must be a woman," Maggie says as she sits on a couch and invites Murphy to join her. He curls up next to her, watching her with adoration in his brown eyes. "Tell me everything."

"It's lack of sleep."

"Spill it," she insists with a grin, showing me the dimples in her cheeks. I never could resist either of my sisters.

"I met a woman at the hospital party over the weekend."

"What's her name?"

"Anastasia."

"That's a fancy name." Maggie waggles her eyebrows, making me chuckle. "So, she hasn't returned your calls?"

"I haven't called her."

"Right. Because you *don't use your bloody phone.*"

"I didn't get her number."

Maggie frowns, watching me as I push my fingers through my hair and pace the porch.

"So, you like her?"

"Yeah. I saw her twice in two days." I tell her about finding Anastasia in my museum, and then again at the party. I even tell her that I took Anastasia back to my room.

"Wait." Maggie holds up a hand. "You *had sex* with her?"

"Yes."

"Wow." She blinks at me. "You don't do that, Kane. I mean, you're not innocent, but you don't make a habit of sleeping with strangers."

"I don't, no."

"And your Irish is showing," she says with a slow

smile. Maggie's always said my accent is thicker when I'm riled up. She's probably right. "You need to find her."

"I don't think she's after being found," I say with frustration. "She left in the middle of the night, while I was sleeping."

"You actually *slept*?"

"Like a bloody baby," I mutter. I never sleep well, haven't since I was a lad. But with Anastasia, I fell asleep and slept like the dead until the sunlight hit me the next morning.

And she was gone.

"You had sex, you *slept*, and you're still messed up over her. You obviously have to find her, Kane."

"How?"

Maggie tosses her head back and laughs, waking Murphy and stopping his snoring.

"You're going to have to join this century and Google her. Do you know her last name?"

"Montgomery."

"What else do you know?"

"She makes wedding cakes."

"Piece of cake. Pun intended." Maggie giggles as she pulls her phone out of her pocket. "Now, since yours is probably dead, you can use mine."

She taps the screen, then passes it to me.

"What am I looking at?"

My sister sighs deeply in disappointment. "Dude, you sound like you're ninety. It's the Google home screen. All you have to do is type her name and *wedding cakes* into the box and see what comes up."

I do as she says, and when I tap the magnifying glass, the screen fills with images of Anastasia, her cakes, and articles that have been written about her.

"What did you find?" Maggie asks.

"More than enough to find her," I mutter and then smile at my sister. "Looks like I have an address for her shop."

"Awesome. So, are you headed there now? I'll stay with Murphy."

"She left, Maggie. In the middle of the night. I'm going to venture a guess and say she most likely doesn't want to be found."

"There's no harm in going to talk to her."

Just the thought of seeing her again, of touching her smooth skin and kissing her soft lips, sets my blood singing through my body.

"Your eyes are dilated," Maggie says, pointing at me. "You definitely have to go see her."

The alternative is staying here, breaking glass, and pissing myself off.

"Looks like I'm driving into the city."

Traffic makes me want to commit murder. I'm not a fan of people, especially when they're all in one place.

That place being wherever *I* am.

I bought my land away from civilization for a reason. I'm not a neighbor that brings gifts. Hell, I don't even have any people living nearby.

I don't shop unless it's for groceries or sand for my glass, but even that is automatically delivered once a week.

Aside from my siblings, I'm happy to be alone. They all call me a recluse, and I won't argue with that.

But then, I met *her.*

I can't stop thinking about her, reliving the other night in my head, over and over again. I've never felt anything like it. I've also never had my feelings hurt as badly as I did when I realized that she'd walked out on me.

If I manage to do nothing else today, I want her to tell me why she left the way she did. That's all I need, and then I'll leave her be.

I finally make my way through the traffic to Bellevue and turn off the freeway, headed toward the heart of the skyscrapers.

Of course, she works in the middle of the hustle and bustle.

I fight for parking, and then hurry down the block to Anastasia's cake shop.

When I step inside, a bell dings, and I take a deep breath, letting the smell of vanilla and sugar greet me.

"Oh, that's a lovely design."

I hear her voice, but I can't see her. There are cakes,

fake ones I assume, on tables, and cupcakes in a glass counter, waiting to be purchased.

"What do you think, babe?" Another female voice.

"I say you get what you want," a man says.

I poke my head around a half-wall and see a small desk with a computer. Anastasia is sitting behind the desk, and a couple sits across from her.

"Can I help you?"

Anastasia looks up, and then her eyes go round. She bites her lip when she sees me.

"I'm here to see you."

The couple turns in their seats to glance my way, but I only have eyes for the gorgeous blonde who owns the shop.

"I'm going to be a while. Would you like to go get a coffee, or—?"

"I'll wait." I lean my shoulder against the wall, watching her.

"I have chairs out there."

"I'm fine here."

A blush covers her cheeks, and I can't help but remember how the rest of her body flushed and came alive under my hands. My mouth.

Anastasia clears her throat and smiles at her clients. "Do you mind if he listens to our conversation?"

The bride-to-be smiles and shakes her head. "I don't mind at all. It's kind of sweet, the way he's looking at you."

"And how is he looking at me?" Anastasia asks.

"Like he could eat you alive," the groom replies, making me laugh.

"Back to the task at hand," Anastasia says, clearing her throat. "Okay, so you like the purple."

She spends the next twenty minutes firming up a plan for the couple's wedding cake. It's a pleasure to watch her, listening to her steer the customers in a direction that's appropriate for their budget and their party needs. She's wonderful with people, just as talented as she is with her cakes.

Before long, the couple leaves, and I finally have her all to myself.

"Kane—"

"You left."

I hadn't planned to lead with that, but it seems that's the first thing to make it out of my mouth.

"I did." She doesn't pretend to misunderstand me, and I respect her more for it.

"Why?"

"Come with me." She locks the door and leads me to the back of the store, the bakery area. "I'm closed for the day. That was my last appointment."

She pulls a cake out of a fridge and unwraps it, then sets it on a round platter.

"Are you going to decorate that?"

"Yes."

"I thought you said you were closed?"

"No more clients coming in, but I'll be working into the evening." She pulls ingredients out of the fridge and a large pantry. "I'm behind, so we'll have to talk while I work."

I don't say anything, just watch in fascination as she competently begins to mix ingredients, not even using measuring tools.

She just *knows*.

"You're not talking," she says.

"It's been three days."

"Yes."

I narrow my eyes. "Why did you leave in the middle of the night, Anastasia?"

"I think it's obvious," she says with a sigh. "Because I didn't want it to be awkward the next morning. I mean, who wants to have the this-was-a-one-time-deal conversation? I knew the score. No need to make it awkward."

"Who was going to have that talk, I'd like to know?" I ask, leaning against the counter.

"We were the only two there," she says.

"Exactly. So, I have to ask again, who do you think was going to have that conversation? Because it certainly wasn't me."

She stops her movements and watches me, blinking slowly. "You weren't?"

"No. Did I give you the impression that I wouldn't be interested in seeing you again after that night? Did I say that?"

"You didn't have to. We barely know each other, and we had a mutually satisfying, spontaneous relationship that I didn't think would progress after that one night."

My hands fist and my belly tightens.

She thought I'd be satisfied with only one night with her? That's absolutely ridiculous.

I circle around the counter and reach for her hand. The moment her flesh meets mine, it's like coming home.

"I wasn't done with you, Anastasia."

"You weren't?"

I shake my head and bring her knuckles to my lips, nibbling them softly. "Not even close. I don't know that I'll ever get enough of you."

How could I explain to her that the minute my eyes fell upon her in the museum, it was like recognizing a part of me I didn't know was missing? I *knew* her, right then and there. It was a kind of knowing that I can't explain, nothing I've ever felt before, but my grandda used to tell me it was the same way for him when he saw my grandmother.

There's no need to startle her, to confess the knowing to her now. We'll get there.

"What now?" she asks.

"Well, I think it's a good idea to get to know each other, that's for certain."

"Your accent does things to me."

I smile and kiss her forehead before pulling her against me, enjoying the way her arms encircle my back and hold on tight.

"It's glad I am that you like the sound of my voice."

Yes, I turned it up a notch.

And I'm rewarded with a low purr in the back of her throat.

"I really do have to work," she says softly.

"Can I help?"

"No." She steps back with a smile. "But you can watch."

"Darling, I have a feeling that watching you do anything at all is about to be my new favorite hobby."

CHAPTER FOUR

~ANASTASIA~

"I'm so full." I moan as I set my fork aside, resisting the last few bites of chocolate cream pie.

"You're not going to eat that?" Kane asks.

"Nope. I'll burst. You eat it." I push it toward him and smile as I watch him eat it in one big bite. "This was really nice."

It's been a few days since our time in my bakery. He didn't stay the night, he watched me work for a while, and then he left, but not before asking me to join him for dinner tonight.

I was surprised when he picked me up and brought me out to a little island about an hour from Bellevue.

"You have a voracious appetite," he says with a half-smile. "I do believe I enjoy watching you eat, Anastasia."

"I mean, that salmon was ridiculous. Is this your favorite place?"

He tilts his head to the side. "Why do you ask?"

"Well, I'm sure there are plenty of seafood places in Seattle. It's just out of the way, that's all."

"I do enjoy the food here, but it's also close to home for me. I'd like to take you to my place tonight, if that's okay with you."

And just like that, my core tightens at the thought of spending the night in Kane's bed.

"It's okay with me."

He grins and pays the tab, then leads me out to his car, a gorgeous late-model Porsche SUV with buttery leather seats. His vehicle reminds me of Kane, sleek and powerful. Fast. Gorgeous.

He pulls away from the restaurant, and just a few blocks away, I see a bar with a neon sign that says *O'Callaghan's Pub.*

"Wait. What's that?" I point to the pub, excitement already settling in my belly.

"An Irish pub," he says with a wink.

"Yes, I can read. But is it *your* pub?"

"My brother would lose his mind if he heard you say that. No, my younger brother Keegan owns O'Callaghan's."

"I want to see it."

He pulls the car over to the curb and raises a brow. "Do you, now?"

"Aye." I laugh when he narrows his eyes at me. "I couldn't resist. Yes, I want to see it. I've never been to an Irish pub before."

"It seems I'm willing to do just about anything you wish, especially considering I had my mind set on taking you home straight away."

"We'll get there." I cup his cheek and sigh when he turns his face to kiss my palm. "But this looks fun. Show me."

He gets out of the car, opens my door for me, and takes my hand as he leads me through the heavy wooden door of the pub. My senses are automatically overloaded with music and laughter, the smell of beer and food. It's like with two steps, I went from Seattle to a tiny village in rural Ireland.

It's absolutely fascinating.

"It's a liar you are, O'Malley," a man says with a loud laugh.

A woman has a fiddle pressed to her neck, and she's playing with her eyes closed as if she can see the music in her mind. Her hair is long and dark, and she's dressed in a simple black T-shirt with jeans. A man plays what looks like an accordion next to her, singing about war and grief.

"Well, my brother left his solitude to grace us with his company."

I glance up at another woman's voice and only catch a flash of red hair and a slim frame before I'm folded in her arms for a firm hug. "I'm Maggie, the youngest and smartest of the family. I'm also the only one born in America. But I know all of this one's secrets, so you just let me know if you need help with him."

"That's about enough of that, Mary Margaret."

She scowls up at her brother and then smiles at me again. "You must be Anastasia."

"I am." I glance up at Kane, surprised that he's talked about me to his sister. Then again, I told both of my siblings about him, so I guess it shouldn't surprise me at all. "It's nice to meet you, Maggie."

"You'll eat those words," Kane mutters, but Maggie just laughs and wraps her arm around my shoulders, guiding me to the bar. She frowns at a young man and his friend until they get up and move to a table in the middle of the pub.

"There now," Maggie says, gesturing for me to take a stool. "Keegan, our brother has brought in Anastasia."

A man down at the other end of the bar stops mid-conversation and hustles over to us.

"Well, hello there. It's fine to meet you." He holds his hand out for mine, and I reach across the bar to shake it. Keegan is tall and lean like his older brother, with the same dark hair and green eyes.

In fact, Maggie also has the green eyes. They must run in the family the same way blue does with the Montgomerys.

Keegan also shares his brother's accent, where Maggie hardly has one at all. Maybe because she was born and raised here in America?

"Pleasure," I say with a nod. Kane sits next to me and slips his hand onto my thigh, giving me a little squeeze.

"What will you be drinking tonight?" Keegan asks.

"What do you recommend?"

Keegan grins. "Well, now that's a personal preference, isn't it? Kane here always prefers a Guinness."

"And I'll be having a pint now." Kane's voice is mild.

"I'll have one, too," I decide. I've never had the beer in my life, but I'm in an Irish pub, and it's an Irish stout, so I'm game.

"It's a process, building a Guinness," Keegan says as he fetches two tall glasses and slips them under the taps. I watch in fascination as he fusses and fiddles, filling the glasses just so, and then slides them across the bar to us. "*Slainte.*"

"It's Gaelic for cheers," Maggie says and winks as she loads a tray up with drinks to deliver across the room. She stops by the small stage and sings with the young man, completely oblivious to the heart eyes he sends her way as she lifts her voice with the melody.

"*Slainte*," I repeat and take my first sip. "Oh, I like it."

"Aye, and you should, or you'd be breaking me heart." Keegan winks and then works his way down the bar again, taking orders.

"My brother has a way with flirting," Kane says with a scowl.

"He's a bartender," I say and laugh. "Of course, he does. He has to sell drinks and run a business. Working well with people is part of it."

"True enough," Kane says and takes a sip of his beer. "It's not a job I'd want to do."

"So, you don't come in when he's short-handed to help out?" I'm grinning at Kane, enjoying him immensely. I can't picture him with a white apron tied around his waist to save my life.

"He'd throw the drinks in the customers' faces with the first complaint," Maggie says as she returns with her tray full of empty glasses. "So, we encourage him to just come in and drink now and again."

"Good idea." I laugh when Kane narrows his eyes at his sister. "Oh, I hardly know you, yet I can see she's right. So, you're a family of artists?"

Keegan hears my comment and blinks at me. "I'm a pub owner, lass."

"Oh, but you build beers like this one, and as you said, it's a process. Not everyone can do it. It's an art. And Maggie has a gorgeous voice."

"I like you," Keegan says with a grin. "If this idiot screws up, I'll swoop in to claim you for my own."

"I'll break your legs," Kane says calmly and sips his beer as if he's talking about the weather.

We're all laughing when the door opens, and a man walks in. Suddenly, everyone stops laughing.

They stop smiling altogether.

"Fecker," Kane mutters under his breath.

I look around in confusion as the faces that were joyful and happy a moment ago turn to disgust as if someone put spoiled fish on their plates.

"Joey, you're back," Maggie says with a happy smile and bounces over to give him a hug. "You didn't call."

"I wanted to surprise you," Joey says, but there's no joy on his face. "You know I don't like you waiting tables here. There's no need for you to work."

"And *you* know I don't like just sitting at home by myself all week. I'm happy here."

Joey sighs and glares daggers at Kane and Keegan. When his angry gaze sweeps the room, he does a double-take on me. His eyes narrow as though he recognizes me. Should I know him? He looks vaguely familiar, but I see hundreds of people every week. Not to mention, my face is all over my marketing materials, so that's most likely where he's seen me.

"Well, get your stuff together so we can go home."

Maggie rolls her eyes and turns to the bar. "Can you do without me for the rest of the night?"

"If I must," Keegan says. "It's a quiet night."

Maggie reaches for a chip in one of the baskets on the bar, but before she can pop it into her mouth, Joey says, "Do you really *need* to eat that, babe?"

She pauses and then shrugs a shoulder. "No, I've probably had too many already."

She tosses the chip into a nearby garbage can, gathers her purse and jacket, and kisses her brothers on the cheek. When she reaches me, she grins and hugs me. "I'm so glad I got to meet you."

"Me, too."

"Mags, we need to go. I'm tired. I've been traveling all day, for God's sake."

"Coming." Maggie joins him, and he hustles her out of the bar, letting the door swing shut behind him.

"I feckin hate that guy," Keegan says as he dries a glass with a white towel. "I've hated him since the day she first brought him home when she was sixteen."

"I take it that's her husband?" I ask.

"Aye," Kane says, his voice hard and full of frustration. "She married him right out of high school, despite all of us telling her not to."

"Probably *because* we all told her not to," Keegan adds.

"He's a spineless arse," Kane says. "You heard the way he speaks to her. I want to feckin punch him senseless."

"And she'd hate you for it," I say, patting his arm gently. "We can't choose who our loved ones end up with."

"Do you like your in-laws, then?" Keegan asks.

"I love my sister's husband, Wyatt. He's a good man. Funny. Obsessed with her, which is awesome. My brother, Archer, is single."

I won't even go into Archer's past. That's a long story for another day.

The music starts up again, another slow tune about missing a boy who went off to war.

"Why do the Irish always sing about death and battles?" I ask.

"Do we?" Kane asks, listening as he thinks it over. "I guess we do. I don't know why."

We stay long enough to finish our beers, and then we say our goodbyes to Keegan and the others, and Kane tucks me into his fancy car.

We drive about fifteen minutes before he pulls into a long, windy driveway, and up to a beautiful house hidden in the trees.

"You can't see it because it's dark," he says as he turns off the car, but doesn't make a move to get out, "but out that way is the Pacific. We're up on cliffs here. My barn is that way." He points to the left. "And this is my home."

"No neighbors."

"No, I bought this and the properties on either side so I'd have my privacy. I wanted space. I like being alone, Anastasia. More than most."

"You didn't have to bring me here."

"That's not what I'm meaning," he mutters, that lilt thick in his voice again. "I'm happy to have you here. But when I was making a home for myself, I knew that I needed solitude. And the cliffs with the ocean crashing on them."

"Why the cliffs?"

"Because they remind me of Ireland," he says softly. "I'm from the west coast of the country, with rolling green hills and cliffs next to the sea. This place is as close to home as I found, and I scooped it up as soon as I was able."

"You're homesick."

"Sometimes."

"And is that what you meant in the museum when I asked you what you were doing? You were remembering Ireland?"

He looks at me now, his face illuminated by the light of the full moon. "I did. That's what I was thinking of when I blew the glass in that room. The water as it hit the cliffs."

"It's my favorite room at the museum," I confess with a soft smile. "Whenever I'm feeling like my muse is a bitch and on vacation, I go there and sit. I look at the glass and breathe it in. And every single time, my muse comes back to me."

"I'm sorry that I was abrupt when I first saw you." He takes my hand and kisses my fingers. "You took my breath away, and I wasn't ready for it."

"I was a girl in yoga pants with my hair in a ponytail scribbling on a pad."

"The intensity in your eyes, in every line of your body, was something to behold." He steps out of the car and circles the hood to open my door for me. Without a word, he leads me through his front door and turns on the lights.

I don't know what I was expecting, but it wasn't this.

The space is full of color. Pillows, art on the walls, rugs on the floor, all full of color. And the wooden accents aren't honey but weathered barn wood in light grey. It's absolutely beautiful.

Not sterile. Not modern.

Cozy.

"This is a lovely room," I say, suddenly shy. I'm in Kane O'Callaghan's house. And we all know where this is going to lead.

He doesn't have time to reply before a big yellow dog lumbers in from the back of the house, his tongue lolling out of his mouth, clearly excited to see his human.

"This is Murphy."

"Oh, hello, sweet boy." Murphy hurries over to say hello, and we both enjoy a good back scratch. "Aren't you the handsomest ever?"

"And he knows it."

Kane takes my hand and leads me up the staircase, down a hallway, and into his master bedroom. The windows are wide and uncovered. I'm sure the view is staggering when the sun is up.

With no neighbors about, there's no need to cover that view.

Murphy followed us, but with a hand command, the dog lays on a dog bed in the corner of the room.

Kane turns on the light beside the bed and then moves to me, walking slowly but purposefully.

"I've wanted you here, in my bed," he murmurs as his hand glides down my arm and he links his fingers with mine. "I've wanted to watch the way the moonlight dances over your skin. Hear you moan as I do things to you."

"I like it when you do things to me."

His lips press to my neck, and I feel him smile at my confession.

"It's a pleasure to make your breath catch. To watch your eyes dilate. You've the most beautiful blue eyes I've ever seen, Anastasia."

"And you have the most amazing green ones, Kane."

He kisses along my jaw. Finally, his lips cover mine. There's no hesitation as he sinks into me, his tongue taking a taste of my lips, his teeth scraping over my skin.

God, I've never wanted anyone so badly in all my life. This man doesn't just seduce. He puts me in a lusty trance. He's introduced me to yearnings I've never had before.

And I'm no virgin.

But being with Kane is *intense.*

He grips the hem of my sweater and tugs it over my head, letting it fall to the floor. My bra quickly follows it.

Before I know it, I'm standing in the middle of the room, naked. And he's still fully dressed.

Last time, he took control and wouldn't let me explore his body the way he did mine. And as wonderful as it was, I'm determined that we won't repeat that this time.

I reach for the buttons of his shirt, unfastening them slowly, one at a time. After each one is loose, I press a kiss to the skin I've uncovered.

"I didn't get to do this last time," I whisper as I pull the shirt out of his trousers.

"Do what?"

"Take my time with you the way you did with me." I kiss him just below his navel. His stomach quivers, making me bold. I push a finger behind the waistband of his pants and feel the tip of his already hard cock. "You seem to be turned on."

"A man would have to be dead to not want to ride you into the mattress right now."

I smile and squat in front of him, slowly lowering the zipper and unfastening his trousers. When they fall down his hips and pool at his feet, his heavy cock falls forward.

"No underwear." I grin up at him.

He doesn't reply, just watches me with those hot, green eyes. His hands are in fists, his whole body tight with barely contained lust.

With my hands resting on his thighs for balance, I

lean in and lick him from root to tip, enjoying the musky taste of him.

"Christ Jesus, I'll make a fool of myself."

He grips only my shoulders and pulls me up, then lifts me off the floor and takes me to his massive bed.

"I barely got to—"

"I'll come too fast," he mutters, kissing my cheek and then my nose. "And I've been without you for far too long."

"It hasn't even been a week."

"Too long," he repeats as his fingers gently pluck at my nipple. Then his hand glides down my stomach, over my pubis, to the part of me that's pulsing with need for him. "You're so feckin wet."

"A woman would have to be dead to not want to have you fuck her into the mattress right now."

His green eyes flash with humor and then passion as he reaches over me to the bedside table, protects us both, and then pushes my thighs wide.

"Watch," he says, and I comply, looking on as he fills me up. "You're incredible."

He covers me, kisses me, and moves in long, slow motions. The rhythm is sweet, and I know he's working to make it last.

But I want him to lose himself.

So I plant my hands on his ass and pull him to me, grinding against him.

"Faster," I whisper against his lips.

He does as I ask, picking up the pace until we're

both panting and moaning, watching each other with rapt fascination. Before long, we both tumble over.

I HAVEN'T OPENED my eyes yet. I know I'm in Kane's bed, and that it's morning because there's light in the room.

I reach over my head and stretch, my muscles a little tight and sore from several hours of enthusiastic sex.

I'm not sorry in the least.

I turn onto my side and open my eyes. Right there in front of me, his nose inches from mine, is Murphy.

"Does your dad let you on the bed?"

He licks me happily but doesn't move a muscle. I rub his ears and kiss his cheek.

"You're a good boy." I kiss him again. "The goodest boy ever."

I laugh when he wags his tail, slapping it hard against the mattress.

"And you're happy, too. I don't blame you, you have a great house and an amazing human."

I realize I'm having a one-sided conversation with a dog and sit up, noticing a note on Kane's pillow under half of Murphy's head.

A-

I've made coffee for you. Good morning, darling.

-K

I grin and slip from the bed. I'm not about to wear the clothes I had on last night, so I find a T-shirt of Kane's and a pair of boxer shorts, then pad down to the kitchen where there's a clean mug sitting next to the coffee pot.

No Keurig for this man.

But there is another note.

A-

There's cream in the fridge, along with yogurt and fruit if you'd like something to eat. I'm out in the barn working. You're welcome to come out whenever you like.

You're beautiful.

-K

It seems the reclusive artist is a romantic.

I set the note aside, fetch the cream from the fridge so I can make my coffee, and then pull out some strawberries to munch on.

I quickly scan Kane's pantry and discover he has all the makings for some muffins, so I get to work pulling together the treats. By the time they've finished baking, and Murphy has talked me out of a whole one for himself, I'm ready to go outside.

I even found a pair of shoes that sort of fit me. I think they're women's shoes, but I'm trying not to dwell on that too much. He has sisters, after all.

I pile the hot muffins on a plate, grab a fresh cup of coffee, and head out the back door, admiring the sunroom just off the kitchen.

"Oh, Murphy, I could hang out back here."

Murphy flashes me a doggy smile, hoping for more handouts, and joins me on the short walk to the barn. I can smell the ocean and hear it beating against the cliffs. The view is breathtaking.

Yes, I could spend some time here.

Smoke billows out of the chimney of what Kane calls *the barn*. I'm sure at one time that's what it was, but it's been remodeled and looks more like an industrial space now. I open the door and slip inside. And stop cold.

Holy shit, Kane's hot when he's working.

And not just because it's sweltering in the barn. He's *sexy*.

"Shut the bleeding door," he yells, snapping me out of my trance. I hastily shut the door and wait as he turns a long pipe with a bulb of molten glass at the end of it. He blows into the pipe and turns the rod again, then reaches down with a thick, heavy towel and rubs it over the hot glass.

I can't take my eyes off the man.

He's sweaty from head to toe, his T-shirt sopping wet, and his hair molded to his cheeks.

It looks damn uncomfortable.

But from the expression on his handsome face, he doesn't give a shit. He's too consumed by the glass to notice.

Murphy and I wait for a while. At first, I worry that the heat from the room might trigger my asthma, but so far, so good.

I didn't even need my inhaler at the pub last night, which makes me happy.

Finally, Kane puts the glass in what looks like an oven, turns off the furnace, which immediately extinguishes the flames inside, and spins to look at me.

"I didn't mean to interrupt."

"I told you to come out," he says simply and walks to me. "You look better in my clothes than I do, and that's the truth."

I feel the blush creep up my cheeks. "I needed something clean."

"If you think I won't collect them from you later, you're dead wrong." He nods down at the plate in my hands. "What's that you have there?"

"Strawberry muffins."

"I didn't have any strawberry muffins."

"You had all of the ingredients for them, so I baked."

His green eyes shoot to mine. "You made us muffins? Out of basically nothing?"

"You make it sound way cooler than it is." I smile when he bites into one, chews, and then moans in happiness.

Murphy whines, so Kane tosses him a small bite.

"These are amazing."

"Thanks." I eat a muffin and nod in satisfaction. "Not bad. Could've used vanilla, but you didn't have any."

"I'll put it on the grocery list then," he says with a smile. "Thank you."

"You're welcome. This is impressive. I've never watched anyone blow glass before."

"No? Well, if you're good, I'll show you later. For now, I need a shower, and we have somewhere to be."

"I can't go anywhere." I laugh as I follow Kane out of the barn. "I don't have any clothes."

"No problem."

CHAPTER FIVE

~KANE~

"Kane, I don't have *clothes.* I guess I can wear the clothes from last night, though, if I have to."

I open the back door for her and lead her to Maggie's room with Murphy happily following us.

"My sister keeps some things here." I open a drawer and gesture to it. "You're welcome to wear whatever you like. Maggie won't care."

"I won't fit into your sister's clothes," she murmurs but leans over to take a peek. "These yoga pants might work."

"You can keep the T-shirt you found in my closet." I kiss her shoulder and then back towards the doorway. "For now." I wink and then point at her feet. "Those shoes are hers, too. She won't mind if you borrow them for the day."

Before Anastasia can reply, I motion for Murphy to

follow me out of the room so she can change her clothes. I eat another delicious muffin and pour myself a cup of coffee. I should take a shower. I'm always a sweaty mess after a session in the barn, but I'd like to get going before it's too late.

I'll shower when we return.

Anastasia walks out of the bedroom wearing Maggie's pants and shoes, and my T-shirt.

"It works," she says with a smile. "As long as we're not going anywhere fancy."

"You look fantastic in anything. Or out of it, for that matter." I brush my lips over hers. "But no one will see you but Murphy and me for what I have planned."

"Do I need my purse?"

"We're just taking a walk."

She opens her purse and takes out her inhaler, then realizes she has no pockets, so I take it from her and tuck it into mine. I have questions about this, but they'll save for later.

"You'll need a jumper." I pass her one of my sweaters, and then we're off, headed out the door toward the sea. "It seems summer is finally finished."

"Yeah, and my schedule would agree," Anastasia says as I take her hand in mine and link our fingers.

"What do you mean?"

"The heart of summer wedding season is finished, so I can take a bit of a breath." She shrugs a shoulder. "I'll still have weddings through the rest of the year, but not typically up to six a week, which is a lot for a small shop like mine." She points to a flock of seagulls off in the distance before continuing. "I'll be busy with holiday cakes, though, and I give myself an extra day off each week as well. I'm excited for that."

I lead her to the edge of the cliffs, a straight shot from the house, and watch her face as she takes in my view.

"Oh, Kane." She takes a deep breath. "This view is incredible."

"This is just the beginning." I kiss her cheek and point to the lane that veers to the right. "We'll take that path down to the beach. The landscape changes drastically about a hundred yards that way."

"I'm game," she says immediately. We turn, and Murphy runs ahead, already anticipating where we're headed.

It's usually just Murphy and I that take this walk each day. I listen to the wind through the trees and let my mind wander while the dog sniffs and plays.

"The trees arc so pretty on the coast," Anastasia says, watching as we catch glimpses of the water through the limbs. "So green."

We reach the sand, and Murphy takes off like a shot down the beach.

"Oh, should we put him on a leash?" she asks.

"He would think he's being punished." I laugh and lead her down the beach in the direction where Murphy ran. "There's no one about, Anastasia. He won't hurt anything, and he's smart enough to not drown himself."

"I have to admit, I have a crush on your dog."

I raise a brow. "Is that the way of it, then? You've a thing for Murphy."

"I always wanted a dog," she admits. "We always had animals in the house when we were growing up, but then I left home, and living in an apartment in San Francisco wasn't the right place for a dog."

I want to know everything, all at once. I want to know why she was in California, what really made her move back to Seattle. I want to know everything.

"He was in bed with me when I woke up."

My head comes up in surprise. "Who was?"

"Murphy."

My shoulders relax.

"He was quite pleased with himself."

"I'm sure he was since he's not allowed on the bed, that mangy mutt."

Her head falls back with a laugh. "I thought that might be the case. He was pleased as punch."

"My own dog, trying to charm my girl."

Anastasia simply laughs and then points. "What's that?"

"Rocks. This whole area is volcanic, or it was anyway. There are lots of places along the coast with large rocks coming up through the sand. It's especially true along the Oregon coast."

"You're quite the traveler."

I nod. "I like the sea. The tide's out now, and Murphy and I like to come down and see what the water left behind."

"Fun," she says as we approach the tide pools. Murphy's already there, his tail wagging, barking at something just under the surface of the shallow water.

"He found a crab," I say with a laugh. "And if he's not careful, it'll get his nose."

"I'll protect you, sweet Murphy," Anastasia croons, rubbing the dog's ears. Never in my life have I been jealous of an animal. Or anyone, for that matter.

But I feel it in my belly now.

I shake my head at the absurdity of it all, and we spend the next hour walking the beach.

"This is where your muse lives," Anastasia says as we walk back.

"You sound surprised."

"I'm honored."

"You told me about finding your inspiration in my museum." We stop on the wet sand, and I cup her cheek, brushing my thumb across the soft skin there. "And if that's not an honor, I don't know what is, Anastasia. I do get some of my best ideas on this beach, that's the truth of it."

"Have you thought of anything new today?"

"I have." I kiss her nose and then begin walking again, but she doesn't move with me. "Are you coming?"

"You're not going to tell me what you thought of?"

"No. I'm not." I soften the words with a smile. "You may see soon enough."

"What were you working on this morning?"

I swallow and look out at the sea. "It used to be that I fired my glass the way I wanted and didn't take direction or requests from anyone. I didn't want to be told how I should make my art."

"I understand that."

"But then things changed. The fame, the recognition, it's something. I have nothing to complain about. Nothing at all."

"You're not complaining," she says and smiles. "You're talking."

I brush my fingers through her silky, blond hair and wonder what I did right in my life to have her in it.

"I've a good job," I say at last. "It's given me more than any one man should have. More than anyone in my family could have dreamed of. It's a poor family that I come from, Anastasia. And the glass has changed that."

"I'm sure they're very proud of you."

"But it means that very little of what I do in my barn is for the liking of it, and more for the duty of it. I make what I'm asked to make. Today, it was a piece for the president."

Her eyes widen, as big as saucers. "Of the United States?"

"Well, in all honesty, he's a former president, but yes."

"No wonder I can't afford you," she mutters and shuffles her feet. "But what did you think of down here on the beach?"

"What did you mean by that?"

"By what?"

"That you can't afford me?"

She smiles, slowly. "Kane, your art is expensive. I would *love* to add a piece to my collection, but when they're up for auction or come up for sale, I just can't do it. Someday, I will. I'll keep selling cakes and save my pennies."

"Feck that, I'll make you whatever you want."

She shakes her head. "No, you won't. I'm not here to get a free gift out of you."

I don't say anything in reply. I'll not argue about this. And I know exactly what I'll be working on in the barn tomorrow, no matter what she says.

My new idea was going to be for her anyway.

"We should go back," I say and whistle for Murphy, who comes running and immediately heads for the trail.

"He's well trained."

"This is routine for us."

We start up the hill, and I notice Anastasia's breathing is more labored. But we're going uphill, and that's to be expected.

"Are you okay, darling?"

"Fine," she says, gasping. "I should work out more."

We climb a few more steps, and then she stops and turns away from me.

"Inhaler." Gasp. "Please."

I pull it out of my pocket and pass it over. She shakes it and pumps it once into her mouth, breathing in deeply. She waits a few seconds and then repeats the motion before turning back to me.

"Sorry."

"For?"

She shrugs. "This, I guess."

"Should we talk about this?"

"No." Her eyes flash as she takes off back up the hill. She doesn't stop again until we reach the top. She's not having difficulty breathing anymore.

"I think we may need to have a short discussion, Anastasia."

"Nope," she says again and won't look me in the eyes. "I'm fine now."

I sigh and take her hand, lift it to my lips, and kiss her fingers. "I'll drop it then. For now."

"When can I see you again?" I pull into the parking space in front of Anastasia's store and turn to her.

"I have cakes on tap tonight and tomorrow, but then I can take a break for a day or so."

"Excellent. I'll walk you in."

She waits as I circle the car to open her door. Once

she's standing, I pin her against the car, pressing into her.

"I don't think I'm ready to say goodbye," I murmur against her soft lips. "I've been spoiled having you all to myself for twenty-four hours."

She smiles. "You can come up for a while. I'll make you dinner if you want. The cakes will wait."

"I don't think I could turn it down if I wanted to. And I don't want to." I linger, nibbling at her, breathing her in. "Have I told you today how beautiful you are, Anastasia?"

"Only like three times." But the satisfaction in her blue eyes tells me she never tires of hearing it.

And I'll never tire of telling her.

"Not enough, then." I kiss her nose—it's becoming a habit—and then pull away. "Let's get upstairs then so I can nibble on you in private."

She laughs and leads me into the building, through a door next to the storefront entrance, and up a flight of stairs to her apartment.

"It seems you're as much of a workaholic as I am, living where you work."

"Oh, this is nothing. It used to be that I put in sixty-hour weeks."

She pauses when she reaches the top step, making me bump into her.

"I called three times."

Everything in me stills at the sound of a male voice. Anastasia steps ahead, and I follow, getting a view of the man.

"I texted and told you I'd call you later."

"Who the fuck are you?" the man says, frowning at me.

"On the contrary. I believe the question is, who the feck are *you*?"

His blue eyes narrow on me. "Is this the glass guy?" he asks Anastasia, pointing at me with his thumb. "I thought you said that was a one-time deal."

I take a deep breath, calming my building temper.

"Clearly not," I say.

Anastasia looks back and forth between us and then rolls her eyes. "You know what? I'm going to let you two have it out in private." She turns to the man. "Don't be a dick." And with that, she walks into her apartment and leaves us in the hall to sort this out ourselves.

"I'm Archer." He reaches out a hand for me to shake. "Montgomery."

Montgomery.

"Her brother, then." I take his hand and meet the firm grip with one of my own.

"Older brother," he confirms, looking me up and down. "And you are?"

"Kane. Kane O'Callaghan."

"Right. So, let me just say this right now, Kane O'Callaghan. I don't care how much money you have, or how cool your glass is, or well, anything. I do care about my family. Anastasia is—"

"Anastasia is a grown woman," I interrupt. "A beautiful, intelligent, talented woman. And with all due respect, Mr. Montgomery, I'm here to tell you that it's with the utmost care and consideration that I plan to treat your sister."

"It better be," he says with a nod. "Do you have sisters, Kane?"

"Aye, two of them. And I'd do anything in my power to keep them safe."

"Me, too. So you understand what I'm saying then?"

"I understand perfectly."

I think of Maggie and that idiot Joey, and how I want to strangle that arsehole with my bare hands every time I lay eyes on him. I know exactly what it is to love my sisters, to want only the best for them. To be sure they're treated with love and kindness.

I have respect for a man who'll stand up for his family.

"Are you close to your parents?" he asks.

"I am. They live in Ireland now, but yes, I'm close to them."

Archer nods and rubs a hand over the back of his neck as if he's weighing his options. I'm happy to wait him out, to see what's what.

"I think you and I could be friends," he says at last, surprising me. "As long as you don't make Stasia cry, and I don't have to break your legs, we can be friends."

I cock a brow and feel a smile flirt with my lips. It's the same threat I often make to my brothers: breaking their legs. "Making her cry out in anything other than immense joy isn't my plan, Mr. Montgomery."

"Call me Archer," he says. "And never mention my sister *crying out* ever again."

I laugh as he reaches for the door handle. "Deal."

CHAPTER SIX

~ANASTASIA~

They walk in, smiling. At least, no one's bleeding. Or swearing.

"Is the dick-measuring contest over?" I ask as I pull a casserole dish out of my cabinet and let the door slam shut a little harder than necessary.

"Don't be angry," Kane says as he crosses to me and pulls me in for a hug. "It's a brother's job to see what's what."

"Well, he's seen," I reply and narrow my eyes at my brother, who's just standing by the kitchen island, grinning.

"Whatcha cooking?" Archer asks.

"Mexican lasagna," I say, resigned to feeding not just Kane but Archer, as well. I'd hoped for a quiet dinner and maybe some sexy time before Kane left for the evening, but it seems plans have changed. "And, yes, you can stay."

"I'm hungry," Archer says.

"You're literally *always* hungry," I reply with a laugh, shaking my head as I pull tortillas out of the pantry and set to work building the casserole.

"Do you watch sports?" Kane asks my brother.

"In my family, it's pretty much required," Archer replies and explains to Kane who our cousin is.

"You're related to Will Montgomery?" Kane turns to me.

"His dad and our dad are brothers," I confirm. "So, yes, sports is a thing in this family. Are you a football fan?"

"I prefer what you call soccer. But, yes, I like American football, as well."

"Rugby," Archer says with a grin. "That's a hell of a game."

"I played for a time," Kane says, and then all I hear is static noise as the two men have deep, meaningful conversations about teams and players and missed shots.

Honestly, I'm not a huge sports person. I love Will, and I enjoy watching him, but the rest of it? Let's just say I don't stay up to watch Sports Center every night.

Just as I pop dinner into the oven and turn around, I find the two of them…gone.

"What in the world?" It's like they're long-lost friends and suddenly attached at the hip. I follow voices to my bedroom and feel my eyebrows climb into my hairline.

Archer and Kane are standing with their backs to the room, at my window, staring out at the view.

They're roughly the same height. Archer is a bit broader in the shoulders, but they're slim and fit. Dark blond hair on my brother, and dark brown on Kane.

But they're standing with hands in their pockets, chatting like old friends.

"I knew I had to renovate this building when I bought it," Archer says. He's giving Kane the grand tour of my apartment. "You should have seen it. It was a mess. Stasia asked if she could rent the space for her shop and apartment, and I wanted to make sure she was more than comfortable. She chose the industrial look for the living space, and I think it fits for downtown Bellevue."

"Agreed," Kane says. "Do you own a lot of properties in the area, then?"

"I do. Mostly commercial," Archer says. "I owned a commercial fishing company and sold it off about five years ago. I decided to reinvest in real estate. It's been a good decision for me."

"Especially in the Seattle area." Kane nods, still looking out the window. "Who did the work here? I like the woodwork. It reminds me of what my builder did in my home."

Archer laughs. "Montgomery Construction. Will's oldest brother, Isaac, owns the business. But it was Mark Williams, another family connection, that did this woodwork. He's talented."

"Aye, and he is. He did mine, as well." Kane shakes his head. "It's such a small world, isn't it?"

"Should I leave so you guys can keep growing this bromance you have going on here?"

They both twirl and grin at me. Archer rolls back on his heels. He knows he's irritating me.

Archer never cares about that.

"You were busy with our feast," Kane says as he crosses to me, takes my hand, and kisses my fingers. "Archer was kind enough to show me around."

"That was nice of him." The sarcasm is thick in my voice. "Dinner will be ready in ten."

"Do you have any cake around here?" Archer asks as we walk back into the open living area. My apartment is industrial with a tall ceiling and pipes and vents hanging down. I *love* this space.

"Not up here," I reply. "But I have some cupcakes left over in the shop downstairs."

"You make cupcakes *and* wedding cakes?" Kane asks.

"No, I buy cupcakes from Succulent Sweets downtown to sell to people who walk in. I hated that, during open hours, I didn't have anything ready to carry out at that moment. And the owner of Succulent Sweets is married to—"

"Another cousin," Kane guesses, making me grin.

"Yes, my cousin, Matt. His wife's shop is *amazing*. I have a part-time helper who happens to live over that way, and she brings them with her in the mornings."

"Will you go get them for dessert?" Archer asks, giving me puppy dog eyes.

"Go get them yourself," I reply. "You have two working legs."

"Isn't she something?" Kane asks with a grin.

"Yep, she's something. A pain in my ass," Archer says but hurries out to fetch the cupcakes.

"I'm sorry about this," I say when the door is closed. "I thought we'd have a few more hours of alone time."

"We will, after he leaves," Kane says. "Unless you'd rather I not stay tonight."

I tip my head to the side. "You want to stay, do you?"

"Aye." He leans in and plants his lips next to my ear. "One more night together might appease me for a few days. I'll just call Maggie and ask her to take care of Murphy."

He says the *sweetest* things. Is it because of the accent that it sounds extra sexy? I don't know. But I'm relieved that he wants to stay, and I'm not even going to overthink it.

"I found red velvet," Archer announces when he returns. "And chocolate. And two lemon, but I already ate those."

"Shocker," I mutter with a wink and walk back into the kitchen. I open my wine fridge, contemplating the contents while the boys start talking about something else. The bromance is strong here.

I guess it could be worse. They could hate each

other. I think of how Kane and Keegan feel about Joey, and I'm immediately relieved to know that, so far, Archer seems to really like Kane.

My phone pings with a text, and I'm surprised to see who it's from.

Elena Watkins was Archer's girlfriend in high school. And when they were eighteen, for roughly nine days, she was his wife.

To this day, I don't know exactly what happened to break them up. It had something to do with her parents and threats, but neither Elena nor Archer will tell me about it. Elena and I keep in touch every few months so she can check in to see how Archer is, and I can relay back to him how she is, if he asks.

Which he never does.

Ever.

Also? Elena always texts from a different phone number and speaks in code as if she's in the CIA or something. She always sends the same exact message, and my replies back are the same as well.

Elena: *Have you been to any new restaurants lately?*

This is code for: How's Archer? Because the man eats more than anyone in the world. Well, besides Will.

Me: *Nope, just the same ol' same ol'.*

And that's code for: He's fine, and everything's the same.

If she has news, she'll reply.

If she doesn't, I won't hear from her again for a couple of months.

Elena and I were close friends in school, and while she dated my brother, but after everything went down, we parted ways. I don't hate her. I actually really like her. I just wish I knew exactly what happened between them, and how to get them back together again.

Because Elena and Archer belong together. That much I know.

Just as the oven dings, signaling that our dinner's ready, Kane has to take a call.

"I'll be right back," he says.

"This has to sit for a minute anyway," I say, waving him off. Kane heads for my bedroom, and I take the opportunity to talk to my brother. "I just got a text from Elena."

His blue eyes widen, and his hand trembles when he rubs it over his mouth, and then he pulls himself together and shrugs.

Why are you torturing yourself like this?

"That's nice."

"Do you want to know what it said?"

"No. Why would I?"

"Oh, I don't know. Because you love her?" I roll my eyes. "Archer, it's been fifteen years. If she's still texting me several times a year to find out if you're okay, she still feels something for you. Why are we playing this game? Why aren't you going after her?"

"It's none of your business, Stasia."

"Bullshit."

"It's not."

"I love you, and you're hurting. Of course, it's my business. You stick your nose into my and Amelia's relationships."

"No, I don't. I have a two-minute conversation to make sure I don't have to kill anyone, and then I chill. You need to chill."

"That smells great," Kane says when he returns from his call.

"Drop it," Archer mutters. "And feed me. I'm fucking hungry."

I dish up dinner, pour wine, and when we're all settled at my small, bar-height pub table, Kane takes a sip of his wine.

"I love this label," Kane says. "Cuppa di Vita Vineyard is just south of Seattle, you know."

"I know." I grin. "Our cousin is Dominic Salvatore."

Kane lowers his fork and stares at me. "Christ, you're related to all of Seattle."

"Pretty much."

Archer laughs and sips his wine. "You'll get used to us. It just takes some time."

"I thought my clan was large." Kane chuckles. "You'll give us a run for our money."

"I didn't think he'd ever leave." I poke my bottom lip out as I plop onto the couch next to Kane and rest my head on his shoulder. "I don't think it's normal to be jealous of a sibling."

"I'm jealous of my dog, darling." Kane laughs and kisses my forehead. "But you needn't worry. I've no designs on your brother."

"Thank goodness." I laugh and boost myself into his lap, straddling his hips. I brace my hands on the back of the couch and lean in to kiss him. Not just a light brush of lips, but a deep, sink in and *kiss* kind of kiss.

Kane growls, plants his hands on the globes of my ass, and stands as if it's the easiest thing in the world and then carries me to my bedroom.

"Your legs are in great shape," I mutter. "You must walk the beach a lot."

"You make me feckin crazy." The lilt is thick, the way it is when he's upset or turned on. And if the ridge poking me in the belly is any indication, Kane is *very* turned on. "T'isn't normal."

"To want to have sex? I think it's pretty normal." He lowers me to the bed, and I arch my back so he can take off my pants. "And I want you, Kane. Right now. Do not pass go, do not collect two hundred dollars."

"Feck the two hundred dollars," he growls as he reaches over his shoulder to rip his own shirt over his head and then tosses it across the room.

It lands on my dresser, over the photo of my parents.

Perfect.

"The wanting for you never ends," he mutters and kisses my neck, down to my chest, and farther yet to my breast. He tugs on my pebbled nipple with his teeth. I bury my fingers in his thick, dark hair. My hips move. My legs scissor.

I can't hold still.

"Now, Kane."

"You've no patience, *mo stór*."

I love it when he speaks in the language I don't understand. He's done it before. I'll have to remember to look up the definitions.

Not that I'll remember the words.

Or even know to spell them.

The fire between us burns. Slick skin and yearning. Hot breath. Nibbles, gasps, and laughter.

And when it's finished, when we're lying tangled in each other, catching our breath, I realize that I've lost my heart to this complicated, sometimes grouchy, intense man.

BEING TOGETHER IS BECOMING A HABIT.

I worked my ass off for two and a half days straight so I could get ahead and close the shop for the next few days. It's good that I'm firmly in the slower season. Otherwise, I'd be a wreck.

I arrived at Kane's house this morning after making sure my employee had the storefront under control.

She was busy selling cupcakes and making appointments for consultations for next week.

Wonderful.

Murphy was ecstatic to see me, and I admit, the feeling was mutual. The canine and I rolled around the couch for a good five minutes. I rubbed him down, gave him kisses, and told him what a good boy he is.

And now, we're settled in the sunroom with a hot cup of coffee, waiting for Kane to finish up in the barn.

"Has he been out there for a while?" I ask Murphy. He just groans happily when I scratch him behind the ears.

I don't want to just go out there. It's not that I'm afraid to, it's that I don't want to mess with his artistic process. Also, I assume that opening the door could damage the hot glass, given the way he yelled for me to close it the other day.

So, I'll sit here with my favorite dog and wait. Kane knew I was coming, so he's expecting me.

I'd love to go for another walk down by the beach, but I don't want to do that alone.

"I haven't seen you in a while," I murmur, rubbing Murphy's soft ear. My coffee is delicious, the view is amazing, and this big canine who thinks he's a lap dog is keeping me warm.

I could fall asleep.

And I must do exactly that, because the next thing I know, someone is pressing kisses to my forehead.

"Hello, darling."

"Hi." I blink my eyes open and smile up at Kane. He's had a shower, which surprises me. "How long have I been asleep?"

"I don't know," he says with a grin. "But when I saw the pair of you snoring in here, I decided to take a quick shower before waking you."

I glance down and giggle. Murphy's on his back with his head in my lap. His belly is fully exposed, ready for rubs and scratches.

"He's a big baby."

"Aye, he is that." Kane cups my cheek. "How are you? I haven't seen you in two days."

"I'm good." I kiss his palm. "I got plenty of work done, and now I'm all yours for a couple of days."

His green eyes soften.

"How are you?" I ask.

"I'm the same," he replies. "I worked straight through. That should keep the vultures at bay for at least three or four days."

"You worked *straight through?*"

"I napped here and there," he says as if it's no big deal.

"Isn't it dangerous working with hot glass when you're not rested?"

"Now you sound like Maggie." He kisses my nose and helps me to my feet. "I'm fit as a fiddle, Anastasia."

I hear a phone ringing and turn surprised eyes up to Kane. "You turned your phone on?"

"One never knows when a beautiful woman might call."

He winks and walks over to answer. I follow slowly behind, touched that he's started leaving his phone on in case I reach out.

I'll have to do that now that I know he'll get the call.

"Where are you?" I hear as I come into the kitchen. Kane turns to me, his green eyes burning hot. "I'll be there in ten minutes."

He hangs up and whistles for Murphy.

"What's wrong?"

"Maggie's car died on her, and she's stranded on the side of the road. Do you mind riding with me to save her?"

"Not at all."

All three of us jump into Kane's SUV, and he drives fast, in a hurry to get to his sister. We come around a turn and see her looking sad and leaning against the rear of the car, her hands in her pockets.

Kane pulls up behind her, and with a smile, Maggie waves and jumps in the back seat with Murphy.

"Thanks for the ride," she says happily. "I was shocked when you answered your phone."

"Why didn't you call Joey?" Kane asks.

"He's in New York for a few days," she says and sighs. "I told him five times that my check engine light was on. I guess he didn't have time to check it out."

"For feck's sake, Mary Margaret, your husband

makes enough money to have you in a reliable vehicle. It's a shame and a disgrace that he doesn't take care of you the way a husband should."

"Kane, I know you love me. Thank you for picking me up."

Maggie pats Murphy's back as the dog settles on the seat beside her, his head in her lap.

We ride in silence for about ten minutes, and then Kane pulls up to a pretty house in a tidy neighborhood where the homes are all different but new. No cookie-cutter houses on this island.

"Why are the cops here?" Kane asks, a scowl on his handsome face.

"I have no idea," Maggie says as we all climb out of the car and walk to the front porch.

"We're looking for Mary Margaret Lemon," one of the two officers says.

"I'm Mary Margaret," Maggie replies with a frown. "What's this about?"

"We should go inside, ma'am," cop number two adds in.

Maggie looks up at Kane, who nods and presses his hand to her back, then looks back for me. He reaches for my hand, I place a hand on Murphy, and we all file into a cozy living room. Once we're all inside, Maggie turns back to the police officers.

"What's going on?"

"We're sorry to disturb you. Is your husband Joseph Lemon?"

Maggie nods quickly.

The police officer's face remains stoic, but he continues. "I hate to be the bearer of bad news, ma'am, but we're here to inform you of your husband's death earlier this morning."

CHAPTER SEVEN

~ANASTASIA~

Maggie's face pales, and she slowly lowers herself to the couch. Murphy hurries to her and lays his head in her lap as if he knows she needs comforting.

"Massive heart attack," the policeman says.

"He was twenty-six," Kane says, shoving his hands into his pockets and watching his sister carefully.

I shake off the shock and hurry to Maggie, sit next to her, and wrap my arm around her shoulders.

She isn't crying, but her hands shake as she pets Murphy and listens as the cops tell Kane about the massive heart attack and that there were witnesses, making it easier to identify the cause of death. Once they give Kane more information about where the body is, they leave, and we're left staring at each other as the stillness of the room becomes deafening.

"I'm so sorry, Maggie."

She sighs deeply, bends over to kiss Murphy, and then slowly shakes her head. "I think I'd like to be alone."

"Not happening," Kane says and hurries out of the room. I hear a kitchen faucet running, and the clatter of dishes and silverware.

Several long, silent minutes later, Kane returns with a hot cup of tea.

"Here, love. Have some tea. Perhaps you should lie down."

"Kane, I'm okay. Honest. I just want to be alone for a while."

"You're in shock," Kane says.

I drop my arm and stand, frowning at the man I've come to love in such a short time.

"She wants us to go, Kane." Let the poor woman fall apart in private.

"She doesn't," he insists. "I have to call the family. We need to make arrangements—"

Maggie stands and takes her brother's face in her hands. She kisses his cheek and then smiles up at him with the saddest eyes I've ever seen.

"I love you to distraction. But I want to be alone now, okay?"

"No, it's not okay, Mary Margaret." He tips his forehead against hers. "I'm so sorry, love."

"Kane," she whispers, her lip quivering, "I need you to go now."

"We're going," I say and take Kane's hand, urging

him toward the door. "Let's head back home. You're right, there's plenty to do."

"I'll make the calls," Maggie says firmly after swallowing hard. "Later."

Murphy stays sitting on Maggie's couch, not moving.

"You stay with her," Kane says, pointing at the dog. "Take care of her."

Murphy lays his head on his paws, watching us all carefully.

Maggie pushes us out the door and shuts it behind us. But when I start to walk down the steps, Kane stops me.

"Here." He holds the key fob for his car out to me. "You go back to my place. I don't feel right leaving her."

I take a deep breath and climb the two steps back to him, then wrap my arms around his back and hug him. I understand that he's struggling. Maggie's the youngest of the siblings, and anyone with eyes in their head can see that Kane's closest to her. He loves her, and she's hurting.

He wants to fix it.

"You can help her by doing as she asks, Kane."

"She shouldn't be alone."

"I don't disagree with you. But she's a grown woman, who just received the most devastating news a person can get. And she asked for privacy. She wants to be alone."

"She doesn't *know* what she wants," he argues, his voice tight with frustration.

"I do." Maggie flings open the door and pins her brother with a hot green stare, tears floating in her eyes. "I love you, but you don't know what's going on in my head. When I say I want to be alone, that's what I mean. If you stay, you'll hover and ask questions and take over because you're the oldest, and that's what you do. But I don't need it. Now, when I *do* need you, I'll be sure to find you."

She's sobbing as she slams the door shut again, and Kane sighs deeply.

"This is feckin ridiculous. She doesn't need me."

"That's not what she said." I take his hand, and he follows this time down to the car. "She said she didn't need you to hover. She said she'll find you later."

He opens the door for me, ever the gentleman even when his family has been turned on its head.

Should I go home? Should I suggest that he take the time he needs for his family and call me when he's ready?

I watch his profile as he drives. His jaw is tight. In fact, every muscle in his body is flexed, in anger or frustration, I don't know. Perhaps grief of his own. I know he said he didn't like Joey, but if the man's been part of the O'Callaghan family for any length of time, he must have feelings about the man's sudden death.

I reach out and take his hand. Before my eyes, he

relaxes. He turns and offers me a quiet smile. It doesn't quite reach his eyes.

Right then and there, I decide I won't back away. I'll stick by him. If he needs distance, he'll ask for it.

"I hate that she's alone," he mutters.

"Give her a minute to catch her breath," I say softly. "I can't imagine what's going on inside of her right now. And she has Murphy with her. Does she have food and stuff for him?"

"Aye, she keeps him often, so she has everything he'll need. I have to call the siblings," he says as he pulls into his driveway. "I know she'll want to call everyone herself, but damn it, they need to know."

I nod, not wanting to interfere. He knows his family inside and out, and if this is what he feels is right, then he should do it.

I sit on the couch in the sunroom as he paces back and forth, talking to each sibling, telling them what he knows—which isn't much.

Joey's dead.

Heart attack.

The other details are slim to none. There are calls to be made to get the body home, and funeral services to arrange.

He has to tell each of them *not* to rush to Maggie's house. She's asked to be alone. But Kane's sister Maeve insists that she'll call, just to see if Maggie will see her.

"Good luck with that," he tells her. "Our sister's stubborn."

For the first time since we arrived at Maggie's house, Kane smiles.

"Yes, we all are."

IT'S BEEN four days since the news of Joey's death, and two since I last saw Kane. I have a business to run, so I came home when I originally planned to and dug into work immediately. Kane didn't ask me to stay. If he'd needed me to, I would have arranged it, but I'm new to Kane's life, and I don't want to try and insert myself where I'm not needed.

Or wanted.

But we've talked each evening. He sounds tired. He's worried about Maggie because she's closed in on herself. She sleeps, she cries, then sleeps some more. Maeve has been with her for four days, and Kane's parents are on their way.

The family is with her.

Kane's full of worry and a sense of responsibility. He wanted to call in a counselor for Maggie, but she refused his offer.

I suggested he be patient with her. Give her a little time. My heart hurts for her. I almost lost my father last year and thought my world would fall apart. I can't imagine the grief of losing a husband.

And I suspect, once the dust settles and they bury the man, she'll have her moments of falling apart.

We all grieve differently, that's what my mama always says.

I just finished placing the final sugar leaf on a fall wedding cake and put the tier in its box when there's banging on the front door.

I scowl and wipe my hands on a towel as I walk through the bakery to the showroom and then hurry to the door and unlock it. Kane rushes inside, instantly pulling me into his arms.

His lips are sure and insistent as he kisses me. He reaches back to flip the lock on the door and lifts me into his arms, carrying me back to the bakery and out of sight of any passersby.

"Well, hello there," I say when we finally come up for air. "I wasn't expecting to see you."

"I couldn't stay away," he admits and then sets me on the countertop before burying his face in the crook of my neck. "You've been gone for days."

"Two," I remind him and gently run my fingers through his hair, trying not to think about how unsanitary it is to sit on this countertop. "Just two days."

"Too bloody long," he mutters and kisses my jawline.

"How's Maggie?" I ask.

"I don't want to talk about Maggie," he says. His green eyes meet mine. They're full of emotion, but what those feelings are, I can't tell. "I don't want to talk about funerals, or bodies, or any of it."

His hands are firm on my ass, rhythmically squeezing my flesh, just this side of too much.

Kane is intense on a regular day, but tonight, he's even more so.

"We don't have to talk about anything at all."

He grins and covers my mouth again with his, nipping and searching, taking and giving back to me tenfold.

I've never been swept up into anything so profound before. So *necessary.*

"Boost up," he says. He has my jeans undone, and when I push up on my hands, he pulls them over my ass and down my legs. He rips the panties as if they're paper.

The next thing I know, he's inside me, the push and pull urgent. His eyes are on mine as he drives himself in and out, and then, without a sound, he closes his eyes and comes apart, taking me with him.

Our breathing is harsh and loud in the small kitchen. I probably have flour on my ass.

And I don't care.

"Come upstairs with me." I drag my fingers down his cheek and smile when he places a gentle kiss on my nose. "Stay with me tonight."

He simply nods. "I already dropped Murphy off with Maggie." He scoops me up, and takes me up to my home, where he holds me all night, and finally falls asleep.

I'VE NOT BEEN to many graveside funerals. Actually, I've not been to many funerals at all. Which is a blessing.

But one thing I'm sure of is that most widows probably cry at their husband's funeral.

Maggie is wearing a simple black dress with black flats. She's surrounded by her family. The casket is made of rich mahogany and is covered in calla lilies.

We're standing in the rain, listening to the priest talk about walking through the valley of death, and Maggie's holding a handkerchief in one hand at her side, but her face shows no emotion as she stares blankly at the casket. There are no tears now. It's as if she cried all of the tears in the world already. She's still pale with chapped lips, and her red hair is wet from the rain since she refused the umbrella offered to her.

Just this morning, I met Maeve and Shawn, the two siblings that I hadn't met prior to today. Shawn looks just like his two brothers, and Maeve is petite with auburn hair the same shade as Maggie's.

Kane's parents flew in from Ireland yesterday to be here for their daughter.

Off to the side, Joey's parents sob in grief, his mother carrying on about her baby, her only child being gone.

Part of me feels bad for them, but the other part sees it for what it is. An act.

The priest says his last words, finishes with an

"amen," and then the crowd begins to thin. Many come to offer Maggie their condolences. Which is awkward because she barely replies, not looking away from the casket holding the body of her late husband.

Joey's parents don't come to say anything to the O'Callaghans. They don't even spare Maggie a glance, which also has me confused. Do they not like her, just as Maggie's siblings didn't care for Joey?

Someone says something to Maggie that has her blinking rapidly. "What?"

"We need to get her home," Kane mutters. Keegan nods, and they flank Maggie and start to escort her to the car, holding her hands on each side. Suddenly, a woman rushes up to Maggie, stopping us all in our tracks.

"You don't know me," she says, her face blotchy from crying, her hands gripping at torn tissues. "I'm Beth. I was with Joey when he died."

We all stop and go still, listening intently.

"I've been with Joey for over a year," Beth continues.

Our eyes all fly to Maggie. Her face doesn't change much, aside from her eyes narrowing on the other woman. And then, to our utter shock, Maggie starts to laugh. She tips her head back in the rain, letting the drops fall on her face, and laughs as if she's just heard the funniest joke ever told.

"Jesus, Mary, and Joseph," Fiona, Kane's mother says, scowling at her daughter.

"Joey was right," Beth yells, pointing at Maggie.

"You *are* crazy. No wonder he was with me. No wonder he wanted to divorce you and marry me."

"That's enough," Maeve says, stepping forward. "You made your scene, and now you can leave."

"She needs to hear it," Beth insists. "She needs to know what a piece of shit he thought she was. How *dare* she play the part of the widow when I'm the one he loved? When I'm the one who was his true partner."

Before we can blink, Maeve advances on Beth and punches her, square in the nose.

"Oh my God!" Beth shrieks. "You broke my nose!"

"And I'll be breaking more than that if you don't get your fat arse out of my sight," Maeve says, her Irish shining through in her anger.

"I'm going to sue you! I'm going to sue all of you. I should get all of what Joey left behind. Not *her*."

"Get her out of here," I say to Kane, who's already jumped into action with his brothers. They physically move Beth, carrying her down to her car. I can't hear what they're saying, but by the time they reach her vehicle, she jumps in it and screeches away.

Maggie's still giggling. Maeve and Fiona try to calm her.

"It's a mess, that's what it is." I glance over at Tom, the patriarch of the O'Callaghan family. His face is lined with age and worry as he watches his sons walk back to us. "And not the best of circumstances for Kane to bring a woman as fine as you around the family."

"We all have moments," I reply with a shrug. "I

offered to stay away, but Kane insisted I come with him today. And I like Maggie, very much."

"Me, too," he says with a kind smile. He pats my arm gently. "Let's get back to the house and out of this rain, shall we?"

"I think that's a good plan all around." I watch as Kane walks right to me, takes my hand, and leads me down to his car. "You don't want to wait for the others?"

"Feck no," he says and opens the door for me. When he gets into the driver's seat, he has to take a long, deep breath to calm himself. "What's wrong with her? She's acting as crazy as that woman accused her of being."

"You know, sometimes, it's either laugh or cry," I admit. "It could still be shock. Grief. Exhaustion. I don't know if she's sleeping well."

"She slept for two days straight," he replies. "And now we have dozens of people coming to *my* house for the wake, and my sister, who just lost her husband, just laughed at the woman claiming to have had an affair with Joey."

"Most people don't go to the wake, do they?" I blink slowly.

"Enough will. Probably because they're curious."

"If that Beth woman shows up—"

"She won't," he interrupts. "She won't be back."

"What did you guys say to her?"

"Let's just say we're quite convincing when we need to be. Beth is long-gone."

"You're a little scary, Kane."

He doesn't smile. He doesn't look at me. He's a ball of frustration and anger.

And then it occurs to me.

"You haven't worked in quite a while."

"Eight days," he says and rubs his hand over his lips. "I haven't had glass in my hands in eight days, and it might kill me, Anastasia."

"One more day," I assure him. "We'll get through today, and then you'll be free to work."

"Thank Christ." He pulls into his driveway. We've beaten everyone else here, aside from the caterers, who arrived this morning to get the food and drinks set up and now move in and out of the house, going about their duties.

Murphy runs out of the open door to greet us.

"Hey, good boy." I rub his back and then kiss his head. "Did you supervise?"

"He most likely begged for handouts," Kane says as he holds the door for me. The living area has been transformed, the seating moved to small gathering places of four or five chairs. Tables line one wall, covered with both hot and cold foods.

Whoever Kane hired thought of everything.

"Sorry, I know I'm late."

We turn at the sound of the man's voice. Kane grins and walks to him, shaking his hand and then hugging him.

"But you're here, and I appreciate it." Kane turns to

me. "Anastasia, I'd like to introduce you to Cameron Cox. He's been my best mate since I was fifteen."

"He can't shake me loose," Cameron says with a smile. He shakes my hand. "Pleased to meet you."

"Pleasure." Cameron is as tall as Kane but broader in the shoulders. His arm muscles, outlined by his long-sleeved shirt, are *ridiculous*. Cameron has *military* written all over him.

He looks dangerous. Like someone you wouldn't want to cross.

"Are you in the military?" I ask Cameron.

"Was," he says and nods.

"And what do you do now?"

A slow smile spreads over his handsome face. "Well, I can't tell you that. Let's just say I still work for the government."

"Okay, then." I nod and hear doors slam out front. "Sounds like the others are arriving. I'll go see if they need anything."

I leave Kane and Cameron to have their testosterone-filled conversation without me. I have a brother and a million male cousins, one of whom is an ex-Navy SEAL. Caleb is intense and surly. Dangerous.

Just like Cameron.

Maggie and Shawn climb out of Shawn's car and walk toward me. Maggie's not laughing now. She looks tired.

"Hey," she says when she reaches me. "Sorry about earlier. It wasn't funny."

"You don't have to apologize to me or anyone else," I assure her as I wrap my arms around her for a hug. "You're a human being, and we all react to things differently. If you need to laugh, you go ahead and laugh."

"What she needs now is some food," Fiona says as she and Tom join us.

"I don't think I'm hungry," Maggie says.

"It's just a little something for your belly," Tom says and takes her hand. "You've a strong mind and a strong will, Mary Margaret. We have to keep your body strong, as well."

They walk into the house. Keegan winks at me and follows them, with Maeve and Shawn bringing up the rear.

"We don't know you well yet," Maeve says.

"Likewise," I say with a smile.

"But I like you," Maeve continues, and Shawn nods. "You're here for Kane and for Maggie, and that means a lot. It can't be comfortable for you."

"I'm holding my own."

"That you are," Shawn says.

CHAPTER EIGHT

~KANE~

"Say that again," Cameron says, his eyes narrowed. We're sitting out in the sunroom, away from the rest of the people who've come to pay their respects. Though by now, most have left. Keegan's pacing, Shawn's standing at the window, staring out at the sea, and I'm sitting across from Cameron.

"She claims she was sleeping with him," Keegan repeats. "That he was with her when he died, and she's been with him for quite some time."

"I mean, are any of us surprised?" Shawn asks, still not turning from the window. "He left for days, sometimes weeks at a time. He was aloof at best, and downright critical and a bully at worst."

"Why didn't I know any of this?" Cameron asks with a scowl. "I'd have killed him and made it look like an accident years ago."

"You're not here," Keegan reminds my friend before

I can. "You're in Afghanistan, or Chile, or wherever you've been for fifteen years."

"I always come home," Cameron replies.

"We didn't know for sure he was cheating," I remind everyone. "We only knew that he was a jerk. But being a jerk isn't a crime. In fact, neither is adultery, now that I think of it."

"Well, it should be," Keegan says fiercely. "She's a good girl. She's bright and kind. Helpful."

"Beautiful," Cameron mutters under his breath, and I find myself studying him more closely.

"Did I miss something?" I ask him quietly.

Cameron just shakes his head. Before I can question him further, the back door opens, and Maggie herself comes through it with Anastasia and Maeve right behind her.

"So, this is where the cool kids are," Maeve says with a grin as she holds up a bottle of Irish whiskey. "Let's have a drink, yeah?"

"None for me," Shawn says as he turns from the window. Shawn is the youngest brother and the deepest thinker. He's quiet but calculating. Perhaps a bit moody, but being an artist will do that to you.

I should know.

I glance longingly toward my barn as Maeve fills the glasses that Anastasia brought with her. I don't want to make a toast. I don't want to salute a man who hurt my sister the way Joey Lemon did.

Before I can, Maggie raises her glass.

"To Joey," she says. "Who turned out to be the slimy piece of shit everyone warned me he was."

She drinks, and the rest of us share a surprised glance before swallowing our own shots.

"A wife should know, don't you think, when her husband is in love with someone else?" Maggie asks the room.

"A man shouldn't be in love with anyone but the woman he married," Shawn replies. "It's not the wife's fault that her husband made the decisions he did."

"Ah, well. It's done now, and I don't even get the satisfaction of throwing him out on his ass." She shrugs a shoulder and holds her glass out to Maeve for another shot. "More."

"Maggie—" Maeve begins, but I interrupt.

"Give her all the feckin whiskey she wants."

Maggie smiles at Maeve, who gives her another shot. The rest of us sit by, stone-cold sober, watching our sister get shit-faced. She's more than earned it, and that's the truth of it.

Maggie's eyes are glassy as she sings off-key when our mother comes out back and finds us here, keeping watch.

"My God, what are you all about?"

"Well, mother dear, I'm getting drunk," Maggie says. "Alone, I guess, because they're all just watching."

"We've an eye on her," Keegan assures our mum. "How's Da?"

"He's asleep in that recliner Kane has in the study,

with Murphy snoring with him. Maggie, my love, you should eat something to sop up some of that alcohol."

"Nah," Maggie says, shaking her head. "It feels too good to be numb right now."

"We've got her," Maeve assures Mum. "You've had a rough few days, with travel and all of this. You and Da should rest."

"Well, everyone's gone now, and the caterers just pulled out, so we'll do that." Mum walks over and cups Maggie's face in her hands, the way she's done with all of us since we were wee lads and lasses. "You're a wonderful, strong woman, Maggie, my love. You have your drinks and sing your heart out tonight. We'll worry about tomorrow when it comes."

"Love you, Mama."

Anastasia has sat by, quietly watching us all, soaking in stories from childhood with a small smile on her gorgeous face. I motion for her to come and sit next to me, which she does, and slides her hand into mine. I lean over to kiss her temple and catch Cameron watching us.

"What?"

"I didn't say anything," he says, but I can see the wheels turning. I'll tell him later about how I've fallen for Anastasia and my plans. But for now, I need to focus on my sister and make sure she doesn't do or say anything to hurt herself while she gets good and drunk.

"Don't get married," she says to me and then looks at each of us in turn. "Don't any of you ever get married. It changes you. Makes you mean. Impatient." She sips her whiskey. "It makes you stay where you're not wanted."

Cameron's hands fist on his legs. His jaw clenches. He's clearly watching her with the eyes of a man who isn't just looking at someone he considers a sister but rather someone he sees as a woman. It's something I need to pay attention to.

"Are you ready to go to bed?" Maeve asks Maggie. Since our parents moved back to Ireland a few years ago, Maeve took it upon herself to be even more maternal than she used to be, and that's saying something. "Come on, I'll tuck you in."

"Yeah," Maggie says with a deep sigh. "I'm really tired."

"I'm sure you are." Maeve holds out her hand for her. "Come on, love."

Maggie walks next to me but stops. I stand, in case she needs me to carry her in. But she just wraps herself around me and holds on tight.

"I'm really sorry," she whispers.

"Whatever do you have to be sorry for?"

"For all of this. For being a pain in the ass."

"*Mo chroi*, you've been a pain in my ass since the day you were born. We will get through this. Go get some rest. We'll figure the rest out as it comes, as Mum said."

She nods and then takes Maeve's hand, letting our sister lead her inside to her little bedroom.

"Well, if that's not enough to break your heart, I

don't know what is," Keegan mutters, pushing his hand through his hair. "I wish Joey were here so I could kill him again."

"Get in line," Shawn says. "Now, all we can do is take care of her."

"I hate to burst your bubbles," Anastasia says, her voice calm but firm, "but Maggie doesn't need you to *take care* of her. She's a strong woman who will heal from all of this. But being here for her, to help and comfort her, is the most important thing of all. She's lucky to have all of you."

"She has you, too," I remind her. "And I'm glad for it."

I FEEL like I've been working on this piece for an eternity. I started it the morning that Joey died, and I haven't been able to get back to it. I don't like leaving a piece of glass for so long. I have a vision in my head of what it should be, and I can't rest until it's finished.

And this piece is one of the most important that I've worked on in a long time. I want it to be just so.

It's a gift.

And it's finally done.

I turn the fires in the furnaces off, set the last piece in the cooler, and tidy up my barn, putting the pipes and cloths away. I wash my hands and am surprised to see it's already almost noon.

I started at six this morning.

I need a shower, some food, and then the gift should be cool enough to deliver.

"Come on, boy," I say to Murphy, who's been snoozing on his bed in the corner. "Let's freshen up, shall we?"

The dog walks next to me to the house, where my parents have been staying. They're currently spending some time with Keegan at the pub, though. Mom's making her famous stew and shepherd's pie for the evening crowd, and Da is helping with fixing a few things.

The pub used to belong to them. They opened it years ago after we moved to America, and when it came time for them to retire, Keegan bought it from them, and our parents went back to our homeland. They were homesick for both the land and the family there.

I can understand that.

I hurry up to my bedroom, strip down, and get into the shower, not giving the water a chance to heat up. I'm still hot from the work, so the cool water feels good. Once I'm finished, I spritz on a little cologne, shave, and get dressed.

"I know, I've let myself go the past few days," I say to Murphy, who's watching me patiently. "It happens when I'm deep in the barn, as you well know."

Murphy barks.

"I'm hungry, too. Let's go see what we have in the kitchen."

I slip on shoes and join Murphy at the fridge, taking stock of the contents. "You know, it's not a bad thing at all to have one's mother about. She leaves things like this for us."

I pull out two meat pies from the fridge and stick them into the microwave. While I wait for the food to heat, I check the phone sitting on the kitchen counter, and wonder when I checked it last. It's been a few days, at least, and I'm not at all surprised to find that the battery is dead. Murphy and I enjoy our early lunch in companionable silence, and then we walk back to the barn to fetch the pieces I finished just an hour ago.

"Ah, they're cool enough." I place them in their box with plenty of bubble wrap and tissue to keep them safe, and then Murphy and I head out to the car. "You'll have to go stay with Maggie for today."

Murphy barks.

"I know you love her. I'll just poke my head in to see how she is."

I pull up to her house, let Murphy out of the car, and follow him to the door. I knock, and Maggie answers just a few seconds later.

Her green eyes still hold sadness, and I'm sure they will for a while yet.

"Hey," she says and opens the door wide for us to come inside. "I just made a sandwich, but I can make another if you'd like some."

"I ate," I say. "I'm hoping you can watch Murphy for me. I'm headed to the city to see Anastasia."

"Of course, he can stay with me," she says and rubs the dog down, making him groan in happiness. "For the night, then?"

"If that's okay with you."

"It always is." She smiles, but it doesn't quite reach her eyes. "Have fun. Tell her I said hi."

"I will." I start for the door and then turn back to my sister. "Maggie, can I do anything?"

"Not today," she replies. "But thanks for the offer. Murphy and I will be just fine."

I nod and leave, worried about her. But Anastasia was right, Maggie doesn't need us to fix anything for her. All I can do is be here for her if and when she needs me.

Traffic is light into the city since it's a Sunday. I'm excited to see Anastasia. It's been a couple of days, and now that I'm through the fog of intense work, I miss her.

But I find myself frowning when I pull up to the curb outside of her apartment.

She's locking the door behind her, loaded down with bags and a box that must contain a cake.

I jump out of the car to help her before the cake ends up on the sidewalk.

"Hey," I say, jogging to her. "Let me help you."

"I have it."

"Where are you going?"

"Why do you suddenly care?"

I scowl. I've completely missed something.

"Hold up." I grip her shoulders, making her look at me. "What's going on?"

"Check your phone once in a while." She's frustrated, and if I'm not mistaken, hurt. "I've called and texted, and I don't like feeling desperate when it comes to a man, Kane. If you're not interested or don't have time for me, just say so, but have the courtesy to—"

"Stop talking."

Her mouth closes and then opens again but no sound comes out. I hurry back to my car and reach for my still-dead phone.

"No battery," I inform her.

"You can afford a new phone if that's the problem. Or learn to plug it in." She pushes her finger into my chest. This is *not* how I envisioned this afternoon going. "I have a family thing to go to today, and I was trying to call or text you to ask if you wanted to join me, but obviously, you don't. You don't even want to *talk* to me."

"Breathe." I lean in and kiss her forehead, my chest aching at the thought of hurting her feelings. But she pushes me away and walks right back into her shop. "Anastasia—"

"I'm not going to have this conversation on the sidewalk."

"It feels like an argument to me."

"I'm not doing that either." She sets her bags on a

table and whirls on me, fire burning in her bright blue eyes. "I'm not a needy woman, Kane. I'm not clingy. Hell, in the past, I haven't even been particularly *affectionate*. Ask Amelia, she's constantly trying to cuddle me, and I tell her to get lost."

She takes a deep breath but continues without missing a beat. "And I *know* you needed a little breathing room after the past week so you could concentrate on work, and that's not a problem for me."

"Feels like a problem."

"But I tried to call, and you didn't answer, and that's so damn frustrating!"

"You know I'm horrible with the phone."

"Well, you were doing better. You were charging it in case I called, remember?"

I wince. "Aye, I remember. And it's sorry I am that I hurt your feelings."

"Oh, don't just turn up that sexy accent and think you can get out of this one, buddy."

"Now my bleeding voice pisses you off?"

"Pretty much." She props her hands on her hips, her breaths coming fast. If looks could kill, I'd be a bloody mess. "Did you spend the past forty-eight hours not even sparing me a single thought?"

And that's all I can take. I advance on her, not touching her but cornering her against the counter. "I've thought of little else, truth be told."

"Well, you could have fooled me."

"Stay here."

I turn and walk back to my car, fetch the box from the back seat, and return to find Anastasia pacing.

"Open the box."

She narrows her eyes on the container, and then on me.

"Open the damn box, Anastasia."

She does as I ask, and when she pulls the bowls out of the paper and bubble wrap, her round eyes find mine.

"What is this?"

"Mixing bowls," I inform her with a proud grin. There are three different colors—teal, pink, and yellow. Happy colors that remind me of Anastasia. "For your kitchen. I made a few sizes, but if you need something else, just—"

"Kane O'Callaghan made me *mixing bowls?*"

She hugs the middle-sized bowl to her chest as if it's a baby that's going to be ripped from her arms.

"He did." I shove my hands into my pockets, suddenly feeling vulnerable. Does her reaction mean that she doesn't like them? "I was working on them when the news of Joey came, and it was driving me nuts that I couldn't finish them. I knew I would make them for you after I saw your kitchen for the first time. You seem to prefer glass bowls."

"I love glass bowls," she whispers, still holding the bowl. "But, Kane, I can't use these. What if I drop one and it breaks? These are works of art. They're priceless."

"If you break one, I'll make you a new one." I walk to her and brush a tear off her cheek. "Ah, darling, what's this about?"

"I feel awful. I was just yelling at you, and then you turn around and give me the most beautiful gift. I've longed for a piece of your glass, and you gave it to me. For my kitchen."

"Maybe I should have made you something more personal."

"This is as personal as it gets for me." She sighs and reaches out to pet the other bowl. "And the colors are just lovely."

"Are you going to put it down so I can hug you now?"

"Not yet. You *made* this."

I grin, completely taken with her, and brush another tear away. "I can't hug you properly with the glass between us, Anastasia."

"I'm sorry I was mad at you," she says as she carefully sets the bowl on the table and turns to me.

"No, you've a right to be, even if I was quiet because I was making something for you." I tug her into my arms and kiss the top of her head. "I lose time when I'm in the barn, Anastasia."

"I know. I do the same in my kitchen. But it has been a few days without a word, and at the risk of sounding desperate, I wanted to talk to you about this thing today with my family."

"I'm sorry. Honestly, I am, and I will do better with

the phone. It doesn't help that we have an hour between our homes, so it's not as if you can just casually stop by."

"Exactly. And you wouldn't have wanted me to because I was fantasizing about punching you in the nose."

"You're quite violent, darling." I kiss her forehead again, and this time, she doesn't push me away. "Tell me about your family thing today."

"It's just a barbeque, but most of the family will be there, and I was going to invite you."

"Am I still invited, then?"

She smiles. "You're always invited."

"Then I'd enjoy it very much."

"Maybe. You haven't met all my cousins yet."

"I'll be on my best behavior."

She smiles, and just like that, everything is set to rights again.

"Now that we've had our first fight, shouldn't we have the make-up sex that goes along with it?"

Anastasia laughs and passes me the cake she had in her arms earlier. "Not right now. We're late."

"Raincheck then."

CHAPTER NINE

~ANASTASIA~

"You know Mark," I say, gesturing to Mark Williams, the contractor that worked on my building and Kane's house.

"Of course," Kane says, shaking Mark's hand. "How's it going, mate?"

"Business is good," Mark says with a smile and then smoothly picks up the child that attached himself to Mark's leg. "This is Hudson. He's two, so he's basically a monster."

"Rawr," Hudson says, making us laugh.

Steven and Gail's back yard is bursting at the seams with people. I remember back when we were kids, this yard seemed huge to me. It *is* a good-sized space, but with this many people in it, it feels much smaller than it is.

Steven loves to garden. Rose bushes and fruit trees are his favorites, and he has paths that twist through the foliage with benches here and there to sit and enjoy the fruits of his labor.

About six men, including my brother and his bestie, our cousin Will, are huddled around the barbeque, handling it like they were born to cook meat on an open fire.

"He's hot." I turn to see Brynna standing next to me with a glass of something pink held out for me. "Margarita?"

"Yum." I take a sip and follow her gaze to Kane, who's currently chatting it up with Mark and his brother, Luke. Yes, Luke Williams, the Hollywood producer. "Thanks."

"So, spill it. How did you meet Kane O'Callaghan, the elusive, super-famous glassblower?"

"You know him, then?" I grin as I take a sip of my drink, still watching the men. I mean, it's hard to *not* watch them. They're prime specimens of the species.

The hot factor at this party is ridiculous.

"Come on, Stasia. *Everyone* in the modern world has seen his pieces. So, spill it, right now."

"You're bossy, Bryn." I laugh and then shrug a shoulder. "I was sitting in his museum one day, just looking for inspiration. And he found me there. Started talking to me."

"Was it love at first sight?" Nic asks, joining us. I blink rapidly. I haven't admitted to *myself* that I love him yet. Surely, I don't look in love.

"No, he was a jerk, actually."

"Thank you, darling."

I whirl at his voice and then laugh before rising up on my toes to kiss his smooth cheek. Damn, he smells good. I don't know what the cologne is that he wears, but it does things to me. And the fact that it doesn't set off my asthma is a *huge* bonus.

"Well, you *were*," I say and pass him my drink to share. "But he made up for it."

"Hey, Kane's here," Archer says with a wide smile. He passes Kane a beer, shakes his hand, and looks so pleased to see him that it has me shaking my head.

"It seems Archer and Kane are having a bromance," I inform the others, who laugh with me.

"Uh-oh," Brynna says. "Here comes Caleb."

"Caleb, I'd like to introduce—"

"Fine," says Caleb, Brynna's husband, holding his hand up for me to stop talking. "I know who you are. And I don't give a flying fuck. If you hurt her, I'll kill you and make it look like you did it to yourself, do you understand me?"

"Well, that's lovely," I mutter. "And unnecessary."

"He's here?" Will chimes in, hurrying over. "Dude, we'll kill you. But welcome."

I can't help but laugh as Kane shakes everyone's hands, his face never losing the confident, almost cocky smile he's had since we arrived.

"You won't remember everyone's names," Amelia assures Kane as she joins us. "Next time, we'll wear nametags."

I stand back and watch in surprise as Kane works the back yard, moving from group to group, introducing himself to everyone and chatting as if he's known them all for years.

"He's charming." Jules joins me, along with Will's wife, Meg. "And don't even get me started on the accent. Don't tell Nate I said that."

Nate is Jules' husband, and maybe one of the hottest, most intense people I've ever met, with his sleeve tattoo and long, dark hair. He's also completely devoted to his wife and daughter, like all of the men in our family.

"The accent is something to write home about," I agree, then nod and gesture over to where Nate is standing with his dad, Rich, and an older woman I haven't met before. "Who's that?"

"Oh, that's the best story ever," Jules says. "You know Nate's mom passed when he was young. Since then, Rich has been all about running his gym and taking care of his son, right?"

"Yes."

"Well, Rich recently met Marion, and she is *amazing*. They both love fitness, and she's finally talked Rich into retiring so they can spend their golden years traveling together."

"Are they getting married?"

"Next spring," Jules says with a beaming smile. "I'm *so* happy for them."

"So, is the gym being shut down?" Meg asks.

"No, actually, a friend of Nic's is buying it. His name is Ben. He and Nic are from the same town in Wyoming."

"Small world," I murmur. "It's amazing how things come full circle and work out."

"Isn't it, though?" Jules agrees. "Our family continues growing by leaps and bounds. Soon, Mom and Dad will have to buy a bigger house."

"Or we relocate family parties," I add. "Because your dad will never give up this back yard."

"You're right," Meg says.

I take a minute to watch the party around me. My parents are sitting with Steven and Gail, laughing and chatting away in the shade with other various sets of parents. Babies and children run around, playing tag or simply chasing after each other, enjoying the warm fall day in Seattle. Teenagers sit in the grass with their gazes glued to their phones, lost in their own worlds.

Just a few short years ago, our family dinners could fit around a normal-sized table. Now, we need a banquet hall.

"Your brain is moving awfully fast over here," Kane says as he takes my hand in his and raises it to his lips.

"Just soaking it all in," I say with a grin. "You looked like you fit right in."

"Your family's kind."

"Yes, the part when several of them threatened to kill you was particularly welcoming."

He laughs, those green eyes shining with humor.

"That's par for the course, darling. I'd expect nothing less."

"Hey, guys." Amelia joins us, along with her husband, Wyatt. Lia offers Kane a side-hug and then sniffs extra hard at his shoulder. "Oh, you smell good. Is that Bleu by Chanel?"

"You've a good nose," Kane replies. "It was a gift from my sister, Maeve."

"Lia knows all about anything that goes on your body," Jules says. "She's kind of a big deal in the world of cosmetics and such."

"Well, then I'm glad you approve."

"It's perfect for you," Lia says and then turns to me with a frown. "But it doesn't bother you? You usually can't do fragrances."

I shrug a shoulder, not wanting to dive into the limitations of my lungs. Despite starting out kind of crappy, today is a happy day.

"I like it a lot," I reply and smile up at him. "Don't stop wearing it."

We chat for a few moments more, and then Kane squeezes my hand lightly.

"May I have a word alone, Anastasia?"

"Sure."

He leads me down the path that winds through the rose bushes, and when we're away from the crowd of family, we sit on a bench.

"What's up?"

Kane takes a deep breath, making me frown. His jaw is tight. Suddenly, he looks...*angry.*

"Why didn't you tell me that my cologne could trigger your asthma?"

"Because it hasn't," I say and cross my arms over my chest. "If it did, I would have said something. But I like it a lot, and I don't want you to stop wearing it."

"I've asked you several times to talk to me about your asthma, and you refuse. I can't protect you if I don't know *how.* Do you have any idea how frustrating it is to know that something could hurt you, but I don't know what that something is?"

"I don't *need* you to protect me."

"For feck's sake, Anastasia, I'm not telling you that women shouldn't vote or should be kept in the kitchen, barefoot and pregnant—although I like it when you're barefoot, and someday we'll get around to the pregnant part. But let me be a man. I'm old-fashioned enough to say that it's my responsibility to make sure you're safe. And I can't do that if I don't know what it is that triggers you."

"Thank you." I rest my hand on his leg and feel him relax, just a little. "Thank you for being concerned about it. Yes, sometimes, things like fragrances can make my asthma bad. But so can breathing in flour or sugar in the kitchen. Hell, a change in the weather can make it hard to breathe. I just have to be careful, and I'm able to regulate how and what's around me."

"I'll not wear the feckin cologne."

"I *want* you to." I climb in his lap and wrap my arms around his neck. "I've loved the way you smell since the day I met you. As long as you don't spray it near me, I should be fine."

"But you'll tell me if you're ever *not* fine. I'll not negotiate on this, Anastasia."

"I'll tell you," I vow and kiss his cheek. "And, later, when we're alone, I'll tell you about the asthma. I just hate it. It's a weakness, and it makes me feel different. It always has. So, I avoid talking about it."

"I've a right to know." He kisses my nose.

"You do," I agree. "Now, should we get back to the others?"

"In a minute. I think I need a moment with you, just like this, before we join them."

"Take all the time you need."

APPARENTLY, at some point during the family barbeque on Sunday, I managed to get roped into a kickboxing class at Sound Fitness, the gym that Nate's father is about to sell. Jules, Meg, Joy, and Nic are all here with me, and Nate himself is helping me with my gloves.

Jules is my cousin, and I love and respect her more than I can say. But her husband is potent. Dear sweet Jesus, it should be illegal for Nate to be this hot.

In all fifty states.

"I don't usually do stuff like this," I mutter, only loud enough for Nate to hear as he secures the gloves.

"And why is that?" he asks.

"Because exercise is one of the things that can make my asthma a bitch. Hence these hips."

"Where's your inhaler?"

"Right here." I nod to my purse sitting on the table next to us. We all just came marching in, dumped our stuff on this table, and got down to business. "In the middle pocket."

"I'll be right here." His voice is as calm as can be. "If you need it, just tell me, and I'll get it for you."

"Thanks."

"But you're not going to need it, Anastasia."

"I'm not?"

"No." He slaps my glove. "Because you're a fucking badass. Now, get in that ring and kick some butt."

"Yeah. I'm a badass." I knock the gloves together and climb into the ring with the others. Jules told us that Nate used to be an MMA fighter, which only makes him hotter. And if he says I'm a badass, well then, badass I'll be.

"Okay, ladies," Ben, our instructor and Nic's friend, says with a grin.

I glance at Nic, catching her attention, and mouth *he's hot.*

I know, she mouths back, and we fist bump our gloves.

Nic's happily married. I'm in a great relationship

myself. But we aren't dead. It's our civic duty as women to check out the hot men.

"Here's what we're going to do today."

"Before you do that," Jules says, interrupting him, "I didn't think you did classes."

"Not usually, but when Nic told me it would be you guys, I took the class."

"He enjoys torturing me," Nic says, blowing a strand of dark hair out of her eyes. "He's been doing it since we were children."

"Are we gonna chit-chat, or are we going to beat each other up?" Meg asks. "I have baby weight to lose."

"Let's do it." I bounce on my toes, ready to get to it. But Meg's baby comment reminds me of Kane casually mentioning that, eventually, I'll be carrying *his* baby. I let it pass in the moment. I didn't know what in the hell to say. It's certainly too early to be talking about children.

I've never even considered the idea of having kids.

It doesn't repulse me or make me want to run in the other direction. So, I'll take that as a good sign.

"Here's how I want you to hit that bag," Ben says, raising his gloved fists and aiming a jab at the bag. "One, two, one-two. Don't be afraid to hit it hard, it can't feel a thing."

We spend a while learning to punch, and the form we should use. My breathing is even and a little fast, but I'm not gasping.

There's a difference between an asthma attack and exercise.

Suddenly, Nate's in the ring with us, moving from girl to girl, straightening each of our backs, helping with form.

When he reaches Jules, he simply crosses his arms over his chest, grins, and watches.

"Don't make me wipe that smile off your face, ace," Jules says, making Nate chuckle.

"It's been a while since we sparred in the ring," Nate says. "We should probably give it another go. What do you say?"

"I say any time, any place," Jules replies, her voice sure and breezy. "I kicked your ass once, I can do it again."

Nate leans in. "Let's not forget who pinned who, Julianne."

He kisses her cheek and walks away, leaving my dear cousin with flushed cheeks, and not from the workout.

"Focus," I remind Jules. "Don't think about the hot dude you're married to."

"Hard not to," Jules mutters and hits her bag extra hard.

By the end of the class, I'm sweaty, panting, and my arms feel like rubber bands, but I'm not struggling to breathe like a fish out of water, and I consider that a *huge* win.

"You totally killed it," Nic says, offering me a high-five as we leave the ring.

"Told you," Nate says with a wide smile. Which is huge coming from Nate, who's always so intense. "You can exercise just fine. You need to find what works for you, and know your limits."

"It felt great," I say and nod as Nate helps me out of the gloves. "Thanks."

"Come by anytime," he offers.

"It's kind of out of the way, but I'll keep it in mind."

"Now, lunch," Joy says. "Because I worked up a hell of an appetite."

Joy recently had a baby, as well, but she looks fantastic.

"How did you manage to do that kick?" Meg asks me. "You got your leg up really high."

We just stepped out into the parking lot. I pass my bag to Nic and do a super amazing roundhouse kick, but my toe snags on the curb, and down I go. My shoulder slams into said curb, and I see stars as pain pings up my neck and down my arm.

"Oh, God."

"Stasia!" Jules kneels next to me. "What hurts?"

"Everything," I mutter. "That's what I get for showing off my Bruce Lee moves."

I try to get up, but my left arm won't move, and it's aching like a bitch.

"I'm calling an ambulance," Nic says immediately.

"I don't need an ambulance." I manage to sit on the curb. "I just wrenched my shoulder."

"It's dislocated, honey," Joy says. "You need an ER."

"You're a doctor," I say, eyeing Joy.

"I'm a veterinarian," she replies with a laugh. "And you're not a golden retriever."

"What good is all that schooling if you can't put my shoulder back in place?" I wince, not sure what to do. "I'm pretty sure it's just sprained."

"Yeah, that's why you're holding it like that," Nic says, shaking her head.

"Meg? You're a nurse."

"I work with kids who have cancer," Meg replies. "I'm not in orthopedics. Come on, get in the car, we'll take you."

"Be careful," Nic says, taking my good arm and helping me up. I hiss when the pain rockets through my body again.

"Jesus, this sprained shoulder hurts."

"She's in denial," Jules says as she helps to put my seatbelt on. "Here, I found an extra jacket. We'll brace it behind you."

The girls get me as secure as possible, and my phone rings.

"I'll get it," Joy says, pulling my phone out of my pocket. "Hello?"

I hear the tinny voice say, "This is not Anastasia."

"No, this is Joy. Hold, please." She grins and holds the phone out to me. "It's your sexy Irishman."

"Oh, good." I take the phone. "Hi, handsome."

"And a hello to you. How was your class?"

"It was great. I totally kicked ass." I moan when Nic hits a bump in the road.

"What's wrong?" Kane asks.

"Oh, I fell after class, in the parking lot, and probably just sprained my shoulder."

"It's dislocated," Joy says loud enough for Kane to hear.

"It's probably just bruised," I insist, not wanting to think about what it's going to take to put my shoulder back in place. That does *not* sound fun to me at all.

"We're taking her to the hospital," Meg yells.

"Which hospital?" Kane asks.

"It's nothing. Honestly, this is a waste of time and money. I'll just call you when we're done."

"Which feckin hospital?" His voice is hard, leaving no room for argument.

"Seattle General," Joy says helpfully.

"I'll see you there." He hangs up, and I scowl at the other girls.

"This is ridiculous."

"Whatever, Kung Fu Panda," Jules says. "You've got a dislocated shoulder. You have to go to the hospital."

"I hate hospitals."

CHAPTER TEN

~ANASTASIA~

I was right. It wasn't fun, even with the good drugs they gave me. I never want to relive it again.

"You can now claim you've had a sports injury," Will says into my ear. Meg called him after they reset my shoulder, and he wanted to speak to me. "You're one of the elite."

"How many injuries have you had?" I ask him.

"Too many to count. Heal up quick, okay?"

"Okay." I pass the phone back to Meg and scowl when I try to shift on the bed. "It aches like a bad tooth. I need more drugs."

"The nurse said she'd be back with something in a bit," Jules says and pats the hand on my uninjured side. She's been holding it since they brought me in here. Joy ran up to see if she could catch Jace between patients, and Nic is sitting in the corner, texting Matt.

"I'm sorry this happened," Nic says.

"It's not surprising," I remind her. "I'm always the clumsy one. I should know better than to try a roundhouse kick without supervision."

Jules laughs, and then we hear an anxious Irishman say, "Where the hell is she?"

"Kane's here," I say and smile at Jules. "He sounds worried."

"Of course, he's worried." Jules kisses my cheek and moves back, ready to hand her post over to my guy. "We're in here."

"It's a bloody maze in here," Kane says as he hurries to me and immediately kisses my forehead, breathing in deeply. "How are you feeling, darling? What can we do for you?"

"Well, it's a combination of rolling pain and a good buzz from the drugs," I admit and cup his cheek. "You didn't have to come."

"Aye, I did."

"Let's go find some cafeteria food," Jules suggests to Nic and Meg, who both nod.

"Yeah, and we'll check on you in a bit," Meg says. "They said they'd spring you out of here soon."

They hurry out of the room, and Kane winces as he notices the sling on my arm. "I don't like it that you're here."

"It's just my shoulder."

"I don't care if it's a stubbed toe, I don't feckin like it."

"I mean, I would have to be pretty extra to come to the ER for a stubbed toe."

His lips twitch, but still no smile.

"It scared the life right out of me, it did." Kane sighs and kisses my good hand.

"Kane. It's my *shoulder*. I didn't almost die. I was only trying to show off my martial arts moves."

"I didn't realize you know martial arts."

"I don't."

He smiles now and actually chuckles. "But before your display of expertise, it's a fun time you had?"

"We had a lot of fun. My asthma didn't even act up." I wince and shift on the bed again. "Why do they make these beds so damn uncomfortable?"

"You know, we never had that talk we said we would the other day."

"No, if I remember correctly, you were too excited to collect on the make-up sex, and we forgot all about the conversation."

"It was worth it," he says calmly.

"There's really not much more to say," I admit. "I've had it my whole life, and it limits some things, including exercise, but Nate reminded me today that I just need to acknowledge my limits and find what works for me. And he's right. I guess these hips of mine aren't a life sentence."

"And what's wrong with your hips, I'd like to know?"

I laugh, and that makes me hurt, but I continue. "I

was working way more hours than any person should when I lived in California. And I think because we were a big kitchen, with so much flour and sugar and spices in the air, along with little sleep, it exacerbated the asthma. I was worried that I'd have to quit baking altogether.

"But I moved here and opened my shop, and now that I'm working more manageable hours, it's gotten so much better."

"Good."

"Do you remember that night at the gala when I had to run into the bathroom?"

He nods.

"Someone walked by *drenched* in some kind of perfume, and it immediately set me off. I needed the inhaler. And when we were walking back from the beach, I was fine until we were going uphill, and I was trying to go fast, and I don't know if it was the humidity or what, but it kind of hit me then, too."

He leans in closer. "And what about when we make love, Anastasia?"

I swallow hard. "Well, I'm definitely out of breath then, but it's not because of the asthma."

He smiles softly and then kisses me gently. "If there's ever a time when we're together that you feel like you can't breathe, or that you're in danger, you just say the word. There's no need to be embarrassed by it, darling. I always want you to be honest with me."

Before I can reply, a nurse comes bustling into the

room with a syringe. "Here's another round of the good stuff before we send you home."

She plunges the needle into the port on my IV, and then she's gone again, just as quickly as she came.

The difference is almost immediate. My lips start to tingle. The pain dulls.

"I'm always honest with you," I say to Kane. "Like right now. You're the hottest guy I've ever met. Even hotter than Nate."

He narrows his eyes. "Nate's a married man, my sweet."

"Oh, I know. But that doesn't mean I can't look at him. From afar. 'Cause I love Jules *and* Nate. He gave me courage today."

The last few words are a whisper. I didn't mean to say them out loud.

"But enough about him. I was talking about you."

"So you were."

"I like your face." I brush my fingertips down his cheek, enjoying the extra burst of buzz gliding through my veins. "And your hair. It's smooth and thick. Feels good in my fingers."

"You'll give me a big head, darling."

"And even if you can be moody, you're sweet. And kind. And I really love your dog."

"It's my dog that you love, is it?"

"Yeah." I sigh. I want to say more, but the doctor comes in with his laptop.

"How are those meds working for you, Miss Montgomery?"

"Pretty good. I feel better, but I'm talking too much."

"That tends to happen," he says with a smile. "Well, we got your shoulder set, and the X-ray shows no fracture, which is good. You'll need to be in that sling for two weeks."

"Fine, two weeks." But then I perk up, suddenly sober. "*Two weeks*? I can't be out of work for two weeks."

"You need to heal," the doctor says. "Sling for two weeks, not lifting *anything* with that arm. And then, after that, you can't lift anything over five pounds for another week."

"My cakes are heavier than that."

"How long until a full recovery?" Kane asks.

"Could be up to three months before she feels normal again. You have to be careful with it, Miss Montgomery. You don't want to reinjure it. I'll prescribe some pain medicine for you for the next couple of days, but after that, you should be good with some ibuprofen. You'll need to follow up with your doctor in about a week." He types some stuff and then closes his laptop and smiles. "And just like that, you're free to go. I hope you're not driving."

"I'll drive her," Kane replies and shakes the doctor's hand. "Thank you."

"*Weeks*," I mutter in disgust. "I have weddings. Other responsibilities."

"If it's the financial strain—"

"It's not," I insist. "I don't even *need* the money. But couples depend on me, and I have a business to run. I guess I'll be calling in some favors. I hate doing that."

"Maybe we can help so you won't get behind," he offers, which only makes me fall for him further.

"Thank you. We'll figure it out. But I don't think I'll be doing much for a few days."

"You'll come stay with me," he says as if he's already decided.

"I'm sure I'll be fine at home."

He frowns. "I'd like to take you home with me. To care for you and look after you. Murphy would like that, as well. My parents are staying with Maggie now, so they won't be underfoot."

"I like your parents," I murmur and then remember I haven't called my own. "Oh, shit. Parents! I haven't told mine what's going on."

"I spoke with Amelia on the way here. She said she'd call Archer and your parents. But I'm sure they'd like to hear from you to be sure you're okay."

I reach out for his hand. "Thank you. I'll give them a call to let them know I'm all right. But be prepared, they'll probably want to come see me. At least, my parents."

"They're welcome in my home any time at all," he assures me. "Now, let's get you out of here."

I've just managed to get my feet into my shoes when the girls come bustling back into the room.

"Headed home?" Jules asks.

"I'm going to Kane's."

"Good, you won't be alone," Joy says and nods. "Get plenty of rest, drink lots of fluids, and take the medicine. It's there for a reason."

"Oh, *now* you want to act like a doctor. Earlier, you refused to put my shoulder back in place so I could just go out for lunch with you guys."

"I'm a freaking *veterinarian*," she says with an exasperated laugh. "Now, do as you're told."

"I'm surrounded by a bunch of bossy people."

"Bossy people who love you," Meg reminds me and smiles. "Will and I will come see you in a couple of days."

"Thanks."

"Matt said to give you a kiss for him," Nic adds and kisses my cheek. "I'm sure the whole family sends their love."

"Now I'm gonna cry," I mutter. "Because of the medicine."

"Yeah, that's it," Jules says with a wink. "The medicine."

"I can't stay awake."

Kane motions for Murphy to join me on the bed.

He's been more flexible on Murphy being on the bed since I've been around. I think it's sweet.

"You need to sleep," Kane whispers in my ear. He kisses my cheek and fusses with the bedding. The drive to his house was bumpier than either of us was comfortable with, but now that I'm tucked into bed with Murphy on one side and Kane on the other, I'm starting to feel better already.

I'm just so damn tired.

"I guess I could use a nap."

"You can't keep your eyes open, and that's the truth of it," he says. "Would you like for me to turn on a movie for you?"

"Sure."

Murphy can watch it. Because I'm pretty sure I'm about to be comatose.

"What would you like to watch?"

"While You Were Sleeping."

It seems appropriate. I love that film. Kane silently pushes buttons on the remote, and before I know it, I can hear the opening music for the movie.

"I'll be right downstairs, darling." Kane kisses my forehead. "If you need me, just call out or text, okay?"

"Mm."

He leaves the room, and I open one eye so I can look over at Murphy, who's laid his chin on my good arm, watching me closely.

"I always wanted a dog to watch over me." My

words are slurred from exhaustion and medication. "I'm glad it's you. You're the best dog ever."

Murphy yawns, and just as the man in the movie falls from the platform to the tracks below, I feel myself slip into sleep.

"I don't want to."

"Why? Don't be silly. Just get in the boat."

I shake my head, looking at the choppy water around us. I don't even know who the person is that I'm with, but I do know that if I get in that boat, I'll be super seasick. I don't want to be miserable.

I don't want to throw up.

"I'm not going."

"Get in the fucking boat."

"No."

"I'll put you there myself."

I'm lifted into the air, and it's all in slow-motion. There's so much water under us, slapping against the side of the tiny boat. It scares me. I want to go home.

"Let me out."

"Shh."

I open my eyes and find both Kane and Murphy staring down at me.

"You were dreaming," Kane says.

"Yeah, it was a shitty dream."

I scowl as I try to sit up, and my shoulder sings in pain.

"Easy, darling," Kane says, helping me up and fluffing pillows behind my back. Once he gets me situated, I notice a tray sitting on the end of the bed, and realize my stomach is trying to eat itself.

"Is that for me?" I ask.

"I thought we'd eat in bed tonight," he says with a smile and motions for Murphy to get off the bed, which he does. But he doesn't go far, likely hoping for a handout or two.

"What did you bring me?"

"My mum made some stew, which is full of vegetables but should be easy on your stomach. She made homemade bread, as well."

"Did she do this for me?"

"No. She made it for the pub. But Maggie dropped it by just a bit ago, so it's still hot."

"That was nice of her." I take a deep breath and watch as Kane expertly sets up a little picnic on his bed. My bowl of stew has a towel wrapped around it, and I discover it's so I can hold it, but then we remember that I can't feed myself, at least not without a table. "I'm an invalid."

"Not for long," he assures me and holds a spoonful of stew up to my lips. "Here you go."

He watches me with those bright green eyes shining in the low light of the bedroom. It's dark now, and I can't help but wonder how long I slept.

"What time is it?"

"About eight," he says.

"I slept for a long time."

"And it's good that you did," he murmurs as he

ladles another bite into my mouth. I grab the buttered bread with my free hand and take bites of that myself.

"This bread is amazing. Your mom's a good cook."

"She's the best," he says with a wink.

"I've always heard that Irish food is bland. But this stew is delicious."

"It's true enough that it can be bland," Kane says. "But Mum learned a lot once she and Da moved us here to the States. She wanted to serve delicious food in her pub."

"And I'd say she accomplished that."

"Aye, she did."

"How long will they stay?" I pass a bite of bread down to a grateful Murphy.

"They were supposed to leave tomorrow, but with you hurting yourself, they decided to extend their stay by a few more days."

I stop chewing and stare at him, sure I've misheard him.

"Why on Earth would they stay for me?"

"Because they're worried about you, of course."

"They hardly know me."

He sets the spoon in the bowl and watches me quietly for a long moment.

"Anastasia, my family cares for you because *I* care for you. It's hardly a burden for me to change their return tickets back to Ireland by a few days."

"I don't mean to sound ungrateful, I'm just surprised."

"Something you'll learn about my family is, we take care of our own. Always. And if you're with me, you're one of us."

"It's that way in my family, too," I admit quietly.

"Then it won't be a difficult adjustment."

"I never did call my parents."

"I spoke with them. Archer gave me their number," Kane says, surprising me again. "You were dead on your feet, and you could barely keep those gorgeous eyes open. I already met them at the barbeque the other day, so they're not strangers to me, Anastasia."

"You're right."

"They said they'd be by to see you in a day or two, once you're on the mend."

"Thank you." I reach for his hand and kiss his palm. "Thank you for all of this. When a girl is as independent as I am, it's hard to rely on someone else. But I'm grateful that you're here to help me, and that you talked to my family for me when I couldn't."

"You're welcome." He takes a bite of stew.

"Is that what you were doing while I slept?"

"Some of it, yes."

"What else did you do today?"

"I worked this morning," he says. "I'm working on a new exhibit for the museum, actually. It came to me a few days ago, and now that I have it sketched out, I started firing the pieces this morning."

"Can I see your sketches?"

His eyes narrow on me as he chews. "No."

"Come on. I showed you mine, you can show me yours."

"I want to show it to you when it's done. Just trust me on this."

"How long will it take?"

"A few weeks. Maybe more."

"Have I told you before how I hate to wait? I'm not a terribly patient woman."

"Well, that's something we have in common then, isn't it?"

"If you know how much it sucks to wait, why are you making *me* do it?"

He laughs and leans in to kiss my lips gently. "Trust me, Anastasia. It'll be worth it."

"Fine." I kiss him again. "I'll try to be patient. Did you finish the piece for the ex-president?"

"I did, and it's already on the way to its new owner."

"Oh, I was hoping I'd get to see it."

My eyes are already heavy again.

"You should rest."

"This is ridiculous. It's just my shoulder. Why am I so damn tired?"

"Because your body is healing. Let it do its thing. You'll be healthy again before you know it."

"Will you hold me?"

I bite my lip, not pleased that I said that out loud, but Kane slips out of his clothes, leaving his underwear on, and helps me lie down. He curls himself around me, kisses my hair, and murmurs sweet words that sound far away as I float.

But I do hear one thing just before I drift off to sleep.

"Goodnight, *mo ghra*." I feel a gentle kiss to my hair before a whispered, "My love."

CHAPTER ELEVEN

~ANASTASIA~

"We're here!"

The room went from silent and still to party-mode in three-point-one seconds. I've been sitting in the living room, watching movies with Murphy while Kane works in his barn. It's day three of the shoulder crisis, and I'm bored out of my ever-loving mind.

I don't sit still well. Never have. But since Kane brought me home, that's all he's allowed me to do.

Which, I admit, is probably best for my shoulder, but not for my morale.

Seeing Will barge through the front door puts a huge smile on my face.

"And we brought food," Archer adds, bringing up the rear behind Meg.

"You didn't have to do that just for me," I say and

manage to stand without wincing. The shoulder aches. Ibuprofen helps. But if I show them I hurt, they'll make me sit again.

I'm sick to death of sitting.

"We didn't," Will says with a grin. "I plan to help you eat it."

"Me, too," Archer says and winks. "Especially the cupcakes Nic sent with us."

"They eat *all the time*," Meg says, rolling her eyes.

"You've been part of this family for roughly six years," I remind her. "You should be used to it by now."

"I don't think I'll ever get used to it," she says with a laugh. I show them back to the kitchen with Murphy on my heels, wagging his tail and greeting the others.

"He's not exactly a guard dog," Archer says and chuckles as he squats next to the dog and rubs his ears.

"No, he's a companion, Murphy is."

Our heads turn to the back door at the sound of Kane's voice.

"We have company," I say and walk to him, offering my lips up for a kiss, which Kane happily gives to me.

"We came to see the injured woman," Will says with a happy smile. "And to bring food."

"Food that he and Archer will no doubt eat."

"It smells delicious," Kane says. "Fried chicken?"

"With all the fixings," Meg confirms. "We were going to bring Red Mill burgers, but the fries wouldn't be delicious by the time we drove out here."

"Oh my God, Red Mill." I close my eyes, salivating at just the thought of my favorite burger place. "I haven't had them in years."

"We'll go then, once you're feeling better," Kane says, kissing my forehead.

"I'm feeling better," I insist. "But he's making me lay low, and it's killing me. I should be baking cakes."

"You should be resting," Meg says, agreeing with Kane. "He's absolutely right."

"Hear that?" Kane's voice is smug as he takes a bite of chicken. "I'm right."

"Have you been icing it?" Meg asks. "Taking the ibuprofen when you should?"

"I'm pretty sure I'm a snowman," I reply and reach for a dinner roll. "I've had so much ice on my body, I'm surprised my shoulder doesn't have frostbite."

"You always were kind of a drama queen," Archer says as he stuffs his face full of mashed potatoes.

I simply flip him off, making him laugh.

As irritated as I am with the whole situation, it's nice to have these three here.

"Amelia was going to come with us," Meg says, "but she came down with a flu bug and didn't want to make you sick."

"I know, she called earlier." I sit at the small table in the corner of the kitchen and pick at my food. "Poor thing. I wish this hadn't happened so I could be at her place, taking care of *her*."

"Wyatt has it covered," Archer says. He and Will are standing over the cupcakes, deciding which ones to eat first.

"You'd better leave me at least two of those," I warn them.

"Greedy, isn't she?" Will asks Archer, who just nods. Kane grabs a plate, muscles his way between the two big men, and nabs three cupcakes, one of each flavor, and brings them to me.

"Here you go, darling."

"Wow." Meg licks her thumb, watching Kane thoughtfully. "Not every man has the guts to get between those two and food."

"I'm defending my lady's honor. And her stomach," Kane replies and laughs.

I share pieces of chicken and bites of my bread with Murphy, and before long, we're all finished eating, and Will and Meg are getting ready to head back to the city.

"How are the girls?" I ask Meg.

"Growing so fast," she says with a soft smile. "And they're ornery, just like their daddy."

"Not ornery," Will corrects her. "Energetic."

"Well, the energy's killing me," Meg says and sighs. "I love them more than I can say, but they're exhausting."

Will brushes his hand down Meg's hair. "Let's go tuck the girls into bed, and then I'll rub your back for you, lazybones."

"I'll take that offer."

"I'm gonna hang back," Archer says, waving them off. "I drove myself."

"Thanks for the food," I say as Will gently leans in to kiss my cheek. "And the company."

"You know I'm always happy to help you eat," he replies with a wink. "And maybe I wanted to see for myself that you're okay."

Will has always held a special place in my heart. "Thanks. I appreciate it."

Just as Will and Meg pull away from the house, another car pulls in.

"The parents are here," Archer says.

"I'm sorry." I glance at Kane, who just shakes his head.

"For what? I told you your family is welcome here anytime."

"It's a lot of people in one day."

"Stop worrying," he replies and smiles at my parents as they approach the door. "Hello, Sherri. Ed."

"We have food," I offer them. "Meg and Will just left. They brought a whole bunch of stuff that even Will and Archer couldn't decimate."

"I'm still here," Archer reminds me.

"Oh, we ate," Mom says and sizes me up, taking stock of the sling. "We stopped by the pub on our way here."

"You did?" I blink at them both, surprised. "How did you know about the pub?"

"Kane told us about it the other day at the barbeque," Dad says with a smile. "So, we decided to try it out ourselves since we were headed this way."

"Your mother is just the sweetest," Mom says to Kane and wraps her arms around his waist in a hug as if they've been friends for years. "She and your father almost have us talked into taking a trip to Ireland in the spring."

"Spring is a lovely time to visit," Kane says. "We own a little inn there, and you're welcome any time, of course."

"I didn't know you owned a whole inn."

"The family does," Kane says with a shrug. "My cousins are the caretakers now, of course."

"Of course."

So, my parents met Kane's parents and are apparently fast friends. Interesting.

I wonder if this is weird to anyone but me. I mean, we haven't been seeing each other for long, and now our families are friends, and well…what happens if we break up?

It'll be awkward for everyone.

"If you guys want to travel abroad, you should consider Rome," I say, almost desperately. "Or Greece. Mom, you've always said you'd like to see the Parthenon."

"Honey, are you okay?" Mom checks my forehead for fever. "You don't sound like yourself."

"Maybe you should go have a lie-down," Kane suggests.

"No. I don't need to lie down."

"Your grumpy side usually comes through when you don't feel well," Dad says around the cupcake in his mouth. "Kane's probably right, you should rest."

"Why is everyone on *Kane's* side today?" I demand. If I could move my left arm, I'd prop both hands on my hips. As it is, only my right hand lands there. "I'm a grown-ass woman. I don't need a keeper, and I don't need anyone telling me when I need a fucking nap."

"Watch your language," Mom says, narrowing her eyes at me. "What's gotten into you?"

"It's a weird day," I say with a sigh. "A very weird day."

We chat for a while more, and then Mom and Dad take off, leaving just Archer, Kane, and me.

Archer's smile has left his face, and it occurs to me that he's hung back because he wants to talk about something.

"Hey, Kane," Archer says, "do you mind if I chat with my sister alone for a bit?"

"Not at all," Kane says. "I need to go take a shower and clean up from the barn. Take your time."

Kane kisses me, and then he and Murphy disappear upstairs.

"What's up?" I ask.

Archer's pacing the living room, not saying

anything at all. He's clearly agitated, rubbing his hand over his mouth.

"I'm listening," I try again.

"It's your fault," he begins, turning to me. "I was fine, hadn't even thought of her in a long time, and then you had to go and bring her up."

"Of whom are we speaking?" I ask, but I know. I just want him to say her name.

"You know."

I shake my head. "Nope."

"Elena, goddamn it." He sighs and drops into the seat opposite mine. "I haven't been able to get her off my mind since that day at your house when you said she texted you."

This doesn't surprise me. The connection that Archer had with Elena was a rare one. What *does* surprise me is that he was able to resist asking about her for so long.

"What's changed?" I ask.

"Absolutely nothing has changed," he growls. "Except now she's stuck in my head, and I can't get her out. I moved on. Had come to terms with the fact that she kicked me to the curb without a word, without giving me a reason."

"Wait, what? You don't know why she broke up with you after she married you?"

"No fucking clue," he says. "I begged her to tell me why, but she just said it wasn't going to work. That was it."

His eyes narrow on me.

"But *you* know."

"I don't know much," I say cautiously. "I don't talk to her often."

"Did she tell you why she ended it?"

I wince and look away from him. I can't lie to him. He's my *brother*.

"Shortly after the breakup, I met up with her for lunch, and she told me that her father threatened her."

Archer's hands ball into fists, his whole body tensing. "With what?"

"He told her that if she stayed with you, he'd make sure you were killed."

"That motherfucker." He stands and paces again, and my heart goes out to him.

"Archer, I thought you knew."

"Of course, I didn't know," he yells. "Give me her number. I'm going to call her right now."

"I can't do that."

"I swear to God, Anastasia—"

"No, I literally can't. I don't have her number."

"You text with her."

"Yes, but it's always from a different number," I reply. "Always the same message, so I know it's her. Probably a burner phone or an app or something. Here."

I take my phone out of my pocket and bring up the last text from her. I try to call the number and put it on speakerphone.

"We're sorry, the number you have reached is no longer in service."

I hang up and watch as Archer hangs his head in defeat.

"Fuck."

"I admit, I feel bad, *and* I'm confused. Why is this such a big deal now? After all this time?"

"I don't know," he says with a sigh. "But now that I know what her piece-of-shit dad pulled, it's a bigger deal."

"You don't want to piss that family off," I remind him. "They're in the fucking *mob*, Archer."

"Her old man died in prison," he says and winces when he sees the expression on my face. "Yeah, I've watched, kept my eyes open."

"I knew he went to prison," I admit. "I hadn't heard he died."

"So, if he's dead, where the hell is Elena?"

"I don't know," I reply. "And that's the truth. But the next time she texts, I can try to get some information from her."

"No. I don't want to wait that long."

"What are you going to—?"

"I don't know," he says, frustration radiating from him. "And I could take you over my knee and beat your ass for not fucking telling me everything you knew in the first place, Stasia."

"Archer, I seriously thought you knew."

He shakes his head, grabs his keys, and heads for the

door. Without another word, he leaves, starts his truck, and speeds away, leaving me feeling horrible.

Kane and Murphy come downstairs to find me crying quietly on the couch.

"What's all this?" Kane asks, gathering me gently to him. "What happened?"

"Archer's *so* mad at me." I sniffle, trying to tame the tears. I'm not usually a crier, even when I'm alone. Shedding tears in front of someone else is a no-go for me. "And I don't blame him. I would be, too, if the situation were reversed."

"What's it all about, then?"

I take a deep, cleansing breath and start from the beginning. "Archer had a girlfriend in high school. Elena. She was a good friend of mine, and as soon as Archer met her, he fell hard and fast."

"I know that feeling."

I take Kane's hand in mine and link our fingers. "Right after we graduated, Archer took Elena to Idaho where there's no waiting period for a marriage license, and they eloped. They were young and in love, and I guess they felt invincible."

"As one does at that age."

I nod in agreement. "Well, little more than a week later, Elena suddenly broke it off. Told him she made a mistake and had the marriage annulled."

"Well, she was young, darling. Maybe she really felt that she had made a mistake."

I shake my head. "I met with her shortly after, for

lunch. She told me that her father threatened to make sure Archer was k-k-killed if she didn't break it off."

I sniff again, and Kane gives me a tissue.

"Her family has mob connections, and her father was arrested a few years later. But Elena *told me* that Archer knew about the threats. She lied, Kane. Archer didn't know anything until about fifteen minutes ago, and he's so mad at me now."

"What brought this all up?"

"Elena contacts me a few times a year to ask how Archer's doing. It's short and sweet, but her way of checking in. And then I won't hear from her again for months. That night that you and Archer were at my apartment, she texted. And when you left the room to take a call, I asked Archer about her. He said he's been thinking about her since then.

"I fucked up. I didn't mean to withhold information. I didn't know I was."

"You were a child yourself," Kane says in a gentle voice. "Anastasia, you were young, and your brother was hurting. You didn't willfully withhold the information. It's not a bad sister or bad friend that you are. And Archer knows that."

"He's mad at me. He stormed out of here, and I hate it when he's mad. He's always so fun-loving and easy-going. I can't stand the thought of him being angry."

"He won't be for long."

"I should go find him."

"He's halfway to Seattle by now." Kane tucks my

hair behind my ear. "Give him time to cool off, and then talk with him. Call him in the morning."

"You're right. He does need to calm down."

"I've been right quite a bit today," he says with a smug smile.

"Don't let it go to your head."

CHAPTER TWELVE

~KANE~

I've just climbed into bed, next to a sleeping Anastasia, when her phone rings.

I reach over her and snatch it up, not wanting it to wake her. It was a long evening of talking, some tears on her part, and worry as well before she finally fell asleep.

I frown at Archer's name on the screen and then answer. "Hello?"

"Kane!" It's my brother Shawn, yelling over the noise of the pub.

"Why are you calling from Archer's phone?" I ask as I turn and sit on the edge of the bed, away from Anastasia.

"I swiped it from him, and Anastasia was the first person I thought to call. He's in a bad way, is Archer. He shouldn't be driving home."

I sigh and resign myself to fetching Archer myself. "I'll come get him. He can sleep it off here."

"The sooner, the better. He's trying to sing, and it's losing us customers."

"I'm on my way."

I hang up and am not surprised to see Anastasia watching me when I turn around.

"What's wrong?" she asks.

"Your brother. He's fine, but he's sloshed as can be at the pub. I'll go fetch him and bring him back here."

"I'll come with you."

"You don't have to, darling. I'm fine going to get him myself."

"He's drunk because he's pissed at me," she says, standing from the bed. "I'd rather help."

I don't argue. She's awake anyway, she may as well ride along, or she'll just sit here and stew about it.

I help her into her clothes. She tries to hide the pain when she has to move that hurt shoulder, but I see it in her eyes. I wish I could soak it into myself and take it away from her.

Before long, we're in the car and on our way to the pub. She's quiet, chewing on her bottom lip.

"He's just letting off some steam," I say, trying to lighten the mood. "He's fine, Anastasia."

"Archer doesn't drink," she says. "Not because he's an addict, he just doesn't like it. So, if he's drunk enough to be singing in a bar, he's really churned up inside, and I hate that."

"Or he just wanted to drink a couple of pints and got carried away."

She nods, but I know she's not buying it. She's worried about her brother, and if the tables were turned, I can admit I'd be the same.

It doesn't take us long to reach the pub and find parking. When we step inside, we both stop cold and watch in horror as Archer, with a microphone held to his lips, sings a horrible rendition of *Danny Boy.*

"What is it with you Americans and *Danny Boy*?" I ask.

"Oh, dear God," Anastasia says and hurries to weave her way through the high-top tables to the little stage. "Archer!"

"Stasia!" He smiles down at her with bleary eyes. "Found a new favorite pub."

"Come down from there," she says, holding up her right hand for him. "You've done enough singing."

"I didn't know I had such a knack for Irish music," he replies as he stumbles down to the floor, much to everyone's relief. I take Archer's arm and help him over to a stool at the bar. "I'll have another beer," he says to Keegan, but I shake my head.

"I do believe we'll be taking you home," I say and slap his back.

"Nah, not ready to go home," he says, shaking his head.

"A water, then," Keegan says, sliding a tall glass over to Archer. "It's refreshing for a singer's throat."

"Okay," Archer says and takes a sip. Anastasia and I flank him, sitting on the stools on either side. As she makes sure he drinks his water, Shawn joins me.

"Thanks," I say to my brother. "How long has he been here?"

"A few hours, at least," Shawn replies. "He was already half-drunk when I got here. I needed a break from work."

"How's that going?" I ask.

"It's going well, actually." He takes a sip of his Guinness and watches me with cool green eyes. "I received a call yesterday from Luke Williams."

"Did you, now?"

He nods slowly. "He said that he ran into you at a family gathering, and it reminded him that he'd been meaning to reach out to me about writing a screenplay for a story idea he has."

"That's awesome."

"I didn't realize Anastasia is related to Luke Williams."

I laugh and then simply shrug. "She's related, by marriage, to all kinds of interesting people. I'll tell you about it sometime. Luke told me that he's been watching your career and would like to work with you."

"Well, he's in luck because I'm between projects right now." Shawn smiles, and then something behind me catches his eye. "You might want to get that chap home. He's in a bad way."

I glance back to see Archer glaring into his water glass.

"Aye, we'll leave now. Keep me posted on the project."

Shawn nods, and I turn just as Archer says, "I'd like to sing a song—"

"Come on, Bono, we need to get you home and tucked into bed."

I take his arm, and with Anastasia following behind us, guide him out to the car. I pour him into the backseat and head toward home.

"I'm sorry," Anastasia whispers.

"You need to stop apologizing for family," I reply calmly. "We've both large ones, and we love them. There's no need to be sorry for it."

She nods, and by the time we reach the house, Archer has fallen asleep, snoring loudly.

"Come on, mate," I say, pulling on his arm. "Let's get you inside to bed. But you need to move under your own power because you're too large for me to carry."

He mumbles but manages to stand on his own steam to walk as I steer him through the house to the back bedroom.

Archer collapses onto the bed, still in his clothes, right down to his shoes. Murphy sniffs him and whines, I'm sure wondering what in the hell is going on.

"He can stay that way," Anastasia says with a soft sigh. "It won't matter to him if his shoes are on or off, and I'm too sore to try and wrangle them off his huge Fred Flintstone feet."

I smirk and close the door behind me. Murphy leads us upstairs, and once we're finally back in bed, snuggled up, Anastasia holds onto me tightly.

"Thank you," she says. "For everything."

"It's been a week," Anastasia says, her bright blue eyes firing at me from across the kitchen. "Kane, I have to go home. I have office work to do and a schedule to look at."

"Can't we have someone fetch it for you?" I ask. "I've a desk you can use."

I don't want her to leave. I've grown too used to having her here, to having her presence in the house. Murphy adores her. Hell, *I* adore her.

"All of my things are in my office at home," she says. "I'll see you in a couple of days."

A couple of days might kill me.

And it's not just the physical connection that has me completely taken with her. Yes, the chemistry is there, but I've not touched her since she hurt herself. I can't take the chance of injuring her further.

It's been a test of my patience, having her next to me each night, and not being able to have my way with her.

But being close to her is enough to soothe me.

Knowing when I'm working that she's just inside has been a balm to my moody soul.

My parents returned to Ireland, and life is going back to normal. *My* normal includes having Anastasia here.

And now, she's leaving.

"I don't like the idea of you driving yourself," I say and decide here and now that I won't get much work done today. "I'll take you."

"Actually, Shawn's taking me."

I take a breath and let it out slowly through my nose. I'm a reasonable man. I've never been jealous of any member of my family a day in my life. But if Shawn were standing before me right now, I'd break his face.

"He has a meeting out my way today."

"I didn't realize you and my brother have been chatting."

She frowns. "He called here yesterday, *looking for you*. He asked how long I'd be staying, and I told him I should probably go home soon. He offered to drive me. I can't believe I'm explaining myself to you."

"I can take you."

"You're busy," she insists. "You've been working so hard on the new pieces for the museum exhibit. There's no need to take a full day off just because I want to go home. Shawn's literally driving that way today. He's your *brother*. Surely, I can trust him to get me there safely."

"There are few people in this world that I trust as completely as I do my brothers," I admit. "And you're right, I shouldn't take the day from work. But I'd rather you not go at all."

Her lips twitch as she walks to me and boosts up on her toes to offer me her soft, plump mouth.

"Thank you for taking such good care of me," she says. She drags her fingertips down my cheek, effectively setting my blood to boiling. "I'll see you very soon. If I can get things wrapped up there, I might be able to come back for a few days."

"I hate that you're so far away," I murmur before I cover her mouth with mine. I sink into the kiss, claiming her without words. "Come back sooner rather than later, darling. Otherwise, I'll have to come find you."

I'VE BEEN in a pisser of a mood all day. My feelings are bruised that Anastasia left, and with my brother of all people. Yes, it's irrational, but a man can't help the way he feels, can he?

After ruining the piece of glass for the third time, I set the pipe aside in disgust and glance up to see Maggie standing inside my barn. She's petting Murphy and watching me with sad eyes.

Upon closer inspection, I see she's added anger to the sadness today. I'm interested in hearing what rose the heat in her temper.

"What's wrong with you?" Maggie asks before I can ask her the same question. "You look ready to go ten rounds with the champ."

"She left me," I mutter in disgust.

"Anastasia? She broke up with you?"

"No, she bloody *left* me. She went home today. Said she has work to do, but she's not to be moving that arm of hers, or she'll injure it again. It was better for her to recover here, wasn't it?"

"So, she didn't break it off, she just went home?"

"Shawn took her," I continue, on a roll. "My own flesh and blood took my woman away from me. Alone in the car with her, all the way to Bellevue. Inappropriate, that's what it is."

"Wait. You think Shawn and Anastasia are having an *affair*?"

"No, I don't feckin think that." I toss a dirty towel into a hamper, harder than necessary. "He just gave her a ride, is all."

"You've never been the type to be such a drama queen," she says, tapping her lip with her finger. "You're not usually so needy."

"I've never had *her* before," I mutter.

Maggie gasps, and her eyes go round. "You're in love with her."

"Well, of course, I'm in love with her." I throw my hands in the air and stare at my baby sister like she's lost her mind. "I've been in love with her since before I even knew her name."

"That's sweet. A little on the stalker side, but sweet. I'm sure she loved hearing it."

"I've not told her."

"Why wouldn't you tell her?"

"Because the time hasn't been right." I was ready to tell her, but then she got hurt. Family has been in and out daily, and just this morning, she decided to go home. "There hasn't been a good moment for it."

"Well, maybe if you tell her how you feel, you won't be so damn grouchy."

I laugh and turn off the furnace. I'm finished for the rest of the day.

"I'm always grouchy."

"No, you're moody. Not usually grouchy."

"Let's go sit in the sunroom and change the subject," I suggest as we leave the barn, lock it up tight, and walk to the house. Murphy bounces next to Maggie, happy to have one of his favorite people here for a visit.

We walk inside, and I go into the kitchen to retrieve two of the Cokes I keep on hand especially for Maggie because she favors them.

"Thanks," she says when I return to the sunroom and pass her one. She's curled up on the sofa with Murphy's head in her lap, the Lab sleeping contentedly.

We sip our drinks, and I wait patiently for Maggie to pull her thoughts together. She's something on her mind, but she'll come around to what she wants to say in her own time.

I've watched several birds fly around the bird feeder in the yard when Maggie starts to speak.

"I've started going through Joey's things," she begins. "Everyone says that I can wait, but I need to get it over with. And at first, it was just the usual stuff like canceling his cell phone line and boxing up his clothes to be donated to charity."

She licks her lips and clears her throat before continuing.

"Then I started looking through his phone and his computer. It took a few days to comb through everything."

"What did you find?"

"Well, first of all, Beth wasn't lying. He'd been seeing her for quite some time. I found emails, text messages, and tons of receipts from things he bought for her or did with her. She lives in Dallas."

"Joey spent a lot of time there."

She nods. "But that's not all. There were other women. I was able to go back *years*, and I could see when he'd start to get tired with someone and move on to the next. From what I can tell, he didn't have affairs with more than one woman at a time, but they never lasted more than about two years. Some affairs were much shorter."

She shook her head. "I can only assume it was a game for him. Like, *how long can I keep this going before*

Maggie figures it out? I found women going back to about a month after we got married."

My blood is boiling now. I want to kill the arsehole. We always suspected but never looked more deeply into it, thinking we were minding our own business and staying out of Maggie's personal affairs.

Well, feck that. We were wrong.

"That's not the worst of it."

"Feckin hell, Mary Margaret."

"There's a bunch of money that Joey went to a lot of trouble to hide," she continues, her voice steady and sure. There's little emotion in her tone as she runs down the list of horrible things she's discovered about her gobshite of a late husband. "Quarter of a million in one savings account in California. Another with more in Oregon."

"Where the hell did he come up with that much money?"

"I have no idea. He made decent money, but not like that. I'm still finding accounts on his laptop. At least there's one thing that Joey never cared to hide or change, and that's his password. He used the same one for pretty much everything."

"And what is it?"

She laughs. "*Maggiemylove2013.* Ironic, isn't it?"

"I've never claimed that Joey was a smart man."

She shakes her head slowly. "No, he was. Maybe too smart. Because he fooled me for a long damn time, Kane. These kinds of secrets are insane. It's not a couple hundred dollars here and there, hidden away for a rainy day. We could be talking about *millions*. And when I called the banks to ask about them, they wouldn't talk to me about it until I sent them the death certificate and our marriage license because he didn't have me listed as a beneficiary."

She shoves her hand into her pocket and comes out with a key.

"And then I found this."

"What's it unlock?"

"I don't know. I think it's a key to a safety deposit box, but I have no way of knowing where or to what box."

"That's inconvenient."

"It's fucking ridiculous," she says, her voice rising and emotion finally moving over her pretty face. "And I'm damn pissed at him, Kane."

"I'd say he did a lot for you to be mad over."

"No, it's more than that. I'm angry at him for *dying*. How dare he get off so easy? He committed adultery over and over again, hid money, made me eat a certain way, dress a certain way, talked down to me. He controlled *everything*. And in exchange, he gets to just *die*? Of natural causes, no less. He didn't suffer. He didn't hurt. Karma didn't have a chance to work on him."

"Is that what you want, Maggie? Would it make you feel better if he'd suffered?"

"Now that I know all this, hell yes, it would." Her lip

quivers now and tears spring to her eyes. "He *should* have to suffer for it. I'm humiliated, and I'm mortified. I've already been to the doctor to get tested for every STD ever discovered. He was out there, fucking all of those women, and then he'd come home and..."

She swallows hard, not able to continue.

"Well, I've had tests to make sure he didn't give me anything."

"And the results?"

"I'm healthy," she says. "Thank God."

"Indeed."

She rubs Murphy's back, quiet as she lets everything churn inside her.

"What now?" I ask.

"I keep digging."

"To what end?"

"What do you mean?"

I stand and pace the room. I think better when I'm moving. "He's dead, Maggie, and digging all of this up isn't going to bring him back long enough for you to kill him again."

"I know."

"So, what's the point?"

She shakes her head. "I need to know everything he hid."

"You'll never know the why of it," I remind her. "Because he's gone, and you can't confront him."

"I didn't know him at all," she whispers. "He let me

see what he wanted me to see. He manipulated me. He *used* me. And I'm not okay with that."

"No. I'm not either."

"And I don't know where this will lead, but I need to *know*. And then I can let it all go."

"Can you?"

"I have to. Because, like you said, I can't kill him again."

"Maggie, did he leave you *any* money at all?"

She bites her lip. "I have a couple thousand in the checking account."

"That'll last you thirty days, tops."

"I'm working at the pub." She sighs. "I'm selling the house. I don't need a place that big. I don't *want* it."

"I'll help you—"

"No." Her voice is firm now. "You won't give me a dime, Kane O'Callaghan. And I mean it."

I don't say anything. Arguing won't change her mind. I'll make sure that whatever Keegan's paying her at the pub is plenty to cover her expenses.

And I'll make some calls. It's time we hired someone to look into Joey Lemon.

CHAPTER THIRTEEN

~ANASTASIA~

I made it a whole twenty-four hours before I couldn't stand being in the quiet of my office any longer. I worked my way through the administrative work, checked in with clients, and made some calls. I even arranged for my assistant to come in full-time next week so I could get back to baking and decorating.

I may not be able to lift the cakes, but I can surely decorate them.

But now, with all of that finished, I'm ready to be back on the island with Kane and Murphy. Before I headed out of town, I swung in to check on Amelia, who is also on the mend from a brutal round of the flu.

I tried to call Archer, but he's either not speaking to me, or he's busy.

I've hardly spoken to him since that night at the pub. The following morning, he was gone when I woke up. He must have called a rideshare. I'm worried about him, but I know he'll reach out to me when and if he's ready.

I turn the corner leading to the driveway to Kane's place and smile when I see the building ahead. This has quickly begun to feel like home for me. I love the view, the house, and although I haven't spent much time out there, I even love the barn.

It didn't occur to me to call ahead. What if Kane isn't here? What if he's at the museum today? Or helping Maggie?

I should have called. But then, would he have answered?

I get out of the car and slam the door shut. My shoulder is feeling *much* better than it did even a couple of days ago.

"Well, if that isn't the most beautiful sight in the world, I don't know what is."

I turn at the sound of his voice and watch with a smile as Kane and Murphy walk my way from the barn.

"Did I interrupt your work?"

"I was done for the day," he says and immediately wraps his arm around my waist, tugging me gently to him for a sweet kiss. "I missed you, Anastasia."

"I missed you, too."

Murphy wiggles his way between us, his tail wagging his whole body in absolute delight.

"Yes, I missed you, too, sweet boy." I rub Murphy's

back and then follow Kane to the house. "What have you been up to?"

"Besides pining away after you?"

I roll my eyes, making him grin.

"I worked. And I had a chat with Maggie yesterday."

"How is she?"

He sighs, then turns to me, eyeing my shoulder.

"What?"

"Are you up for a walk down on the beach?"

"Absolutely."

"I don't want it to hurt you."

"I'm feeling much better, but I'll be careful."

Kane nods and motions for Murphy to run ahead down the path. The dog barks with excitement and then races ahead.

"He sure loves to play on the beach."

Kane nods and takes my right hand, leading me down the path behind Murphy. He begins to tell me about his talk with Maggie. About the lies and the affairs. Hiding money and more lies. When we've reached the beach, and he's filled me in completely, all I can do is stare at the water as it crashes on the sand.

"Wow."

"Aye."

"Poor Maggie."

"Well, she was good and pissed yesterday, but the grief is there, as well," he says and takes my hand to walk with me down the beach. "She'll heal. It'll take time."

"My heart hurts for her," I admit and take a deep breath, enjoying the way the salty air feels in my lungs. "I'll have to call her and see if she needs anything."

He stops walking and turns me to him, then cups my face in his hands.

"You're a good woman, Anastasia."

"I have moments." I smile, but he doesn't follow suit. His green eyes are sober as they peruse my face, as if he's taking in every line, every detail. "What's wrong?"

"Nothing's wrong at all. I just want—"

"Bark! Bark!"

We're interrupted by Murphy, who's losing his ever-loving mind over at the tide pool, barking, snarling, and jumping about.

"What's wrong with him?" I ask.

"I don't know," Kane says, walking away quickly toward his dog. I can't run, as the motion jars my shoulder, but I hurry behind him and come to a stop beside Kane, staring down at…

"A baby seal?" I ask in surprise.

It's hunkered down in the water, afraid of Murphy barking right in its face.

"Aye, it's okay, little love." Kane snaps his fingers, and Murphy immediately stops barking.

"Come here, boy," I call, urging the dog away from the frightened seal, hoping that Kane can do something with it.

"We should leave it," Kane says.

"But it's a baby."

"Newly born, that's the truth," he says.

"We can't just *leave* it."

"I'm sure its mother is around here somewhere. Murphy likely scared her off. If we leave, she'll come collect her little one."

"We don't know that. What if he's lost? What if the mom is dead? What if he's all alone? Oh my God, Kane, we have to *do* something."

He stops and stares at me. "Anastasia, look."

He points off in the water. It takes a moment, but a little head pops up, breaching the surface, and a seal face watches us.

"Aw, the mama."

"We need to leave them be," Kane says again and motions for Murphy to go back up the trail toward home.

This time, I'm determined to take my time up the hill. I don't have my purse or my inhaler on me, and there's no need to try and impress anyone.

Being slow isn't something to be ashamed of.

At least, that's what I keep telling myself.

But, halfway up, I feel the familiar heaviness start to set into my lungs, and I have a moment of panic.

I don't have my inhaler.

I'm at least ten minutes from the house. That's too far.

"Here."

I blink in surprise as Kane holds out an inhaler for

me. I take it and take a puff. When I can talk again, I say, "Where did this come from?"

"My pocket."

I frown.

"I want to be prepared." He takes it back and tucks it into his pocket once more. "I'll always have a spare on me, just in case."

And with that, he walks up the hill toward home. I can't help but think about how incredibly sweet Kane is. For someone as moody and *intense* as he can be at times, he's the most thoughtful man I've ever been with.

It's no wonder I'm head over heels in love with him.

IT'S dark when I wake up. When we returned to the house, Kane suggested we lie on the bed and watch a movie, which I could never say no to. Spending a few hours in Kane's arms? Yes, please.

Which is actually really funny because I'm so *not* a physically affectionate person. However, when it comes to Kane and his lean body, strong arms, and muscles for days on end, I can't seem to get enough. His hands are working man's hands, a bit rough from all of the work in the barn, but so strong.

And what they do to me when he drags them all over me could quite possibly be illegal.

But I'm not calling the cops.

I turn, relieved that my shoulder doesn't hurt at all, so I can watch Kane in slumber. I don't think he sleeps well usually, but when he's with me, he sleeps like a baby.

He's been incredible since I hurt my shoulder. His patience with me when I was whiny and grouchy was amazing. He's gentle and kind. And he hasn't initiated sex even once since that day.

I know he's afraid of hurting me. Kane wouldn't hurt me for anything in the world.

But, damn it, I'm a woman with *needs*. And the shoulder is good enough that I shouldn't wrench it out again just by having sex.

I mean, I guess I *could*. But we don't have to be that acrobatic.

We'll save that for later.

Kane's wearing nothing under the covers but his boxer briefs. They're white with black trim, and they hug his thighs and ass in the most delicious way.

Glasswork is physically demanding. Kane's body is a work of art in and of itself, and is clearly honed perfectly so he can conquer his craft.

But the eye candy is a wonderful side benefit.

I plant an open-mouthed kiss to his abdomen, just below his navel, then look up to see if he wakes up.

He doesn't.

He has one arm slung over his head. His hair looks darker against the white bedsheets. When I place another kiss, closer to the waistband of his shorts this time, his legs move just a bit.

Enjoying myself immensely, I drag my tongue over the smooth skin just above the elastic and then gently pull them down, exposing more flesh.

His cock grows with each touch of my lips. His skin heats. When I glance up, his eyes are open, bright green, and watching me intently.

"Raise up," I whisper. When he complies, I work the shorts over his hips and down his legs. His cock lays heavy against his stomach, just waiting for me to do all kinds of wicked things to it.

And so, I do. I lick and nibble up and down the length of the shaft, and when I finally wrap my lips around the tip, Kane's hips jerk in response.

"Feckin hell," he whispers, Ireland thick in his voice. "You'll bring me to my bleeding knees, Anastasia."

"No need for that." I cup his balls and gently massage the smooth skin just under them, and watch in wonder as Kane proceeds to fall apart in my hands.

His thighs tense, his hands fist in the sheets, and he bares his teeth.

"Christ in Heaven."

I can't stand it anymore. I need to feel him inside me. I want to ride him until neither of us can see straight.

I gently work my T-shirt and yoga shorts off, then reach over Kane for the drawer with the condoms, and torture us both by slowly rolling it down his shaft.

"I might die," he growls.

With a smile of immense female satisfaction, I straddle Kane's hips and slowly lower myself onto him. My head falls back in delight, and with one hand braced on his chest, I begin to move. Slowly, up and down, our eyes locked.

I bear down and clench around him, relishing how incredible he feels inside of me.

Suddenly, he sits up, locks his lips onto mine, and wraps an arm around my back. He swiftly reverses our position, and I'm suddenly looking up at him as I hitch my legs higher up on his hips, opening myself to him even more than before.

"Anastasia," he whispers. "*Mo ghrá.*"

The lovemaking is slow but intense. Full of soft sighs and deep kisses. Smiles and nibbles.

Before long, we're lost in each other as we fall over the edge into oblivion.

We didn't have sex. I don't know that we've *ever* simply had sex. This is love, pure and simple.

"Did I hurt you?" he asks and kisses the ball of my hurt shoulder.

"Not even a little," I assure him. "I'm feeling much better."

"I'm glad. Because keeping my hands to myself has been torture."

I smile and drag my fingers through his thick hair. "There's no need to keep your hands to yourself. In fact, I rather like it when you don't."

DREAM WITH ME

"Do you, now?" He nuzzles my nose with his and licks my bottom lip before plundering my mouth with the energy of a man who didn't just have mind-blowing sex. "Well, I've a mind to keep my hands on you for a while yet."

"You do have the best ideas."

WE'VE BEEN in this bed for well over fifteen hours, and it's been the best hours of my life. My body feels sated, my muscles sore but deliciously so. I woke up just a few moments ago, alone. But I can hear Kane downstairs, and I can smell coffee.

Bless him.

I put a T-shirt on but nothing else and walk downstairs in search of my man—and the promised java.

"Thank goodness you got the coffee started. I'm going to need extra caffeine after all that—"

I stop cold, mortified to see both Shawn and Keegan standing in Kane's kitchen with him, each with a mug of coffee in hand.

Kane's mug is halfway to his mouth, but it stops there as his eyes roam up and down my body and widen.

I glance down.

I'm only in a thin, white T-shirt that barely covers my crotch and leaves nothing to the imagination with the way you can see my dark nipples through the fabric.

"Well," I say and clear my throat. "Here we are."

Kane rushes into the mudroom and returns with a big flannel shirt and wraps it around me, covering me from the others.

"If you both don't stop looking at her, I'll burn your bloody eyes out of your head."

Both Keegan and Shawn are laughing now, and my face feels like it's hotter than the furnaces out in the barn.

"I thought you were down here making coffee," I say lamely.

"I was," he replies. "And when I left you, you were sound asleep."

"I woke up."

"So I see. We have company."

I laugh now, unable to keep the giggles under control. "So *I* see. Why don't I go upstairs and get dressed, and then I'll come down and have coffee with you all in a civilized manner?"

"I would prefer that, yes," Kane says. He kisses me on the forehead before I turn around, and he slaps me smartly on the ass. "Cover that gorgeous body up, please."

"Yes, sir."

I can hear the guys laughing as I climb the stairs, and then I hear another car door slam.

I had no idea that we would be grand central station this morning. Someone could have warned me.

I hurry into jeans and a loose top, brush my hair, and wash my face, feeling more like myself when I walk downstairs and see that Maeve has joined her brothers in the kitchen.

"I hear you just put on quite the show," she says with a smile.

"In my defense, I thought we were alone," I reply. "They weren't even talking or anything."

"We were enjoying the first sips of caffeine," Keegan says and winks. "But no need to worry. We didn't see anything."

"What's the party for?" I ask as Kane passes me my mug full of wonderful coffee. "And where's Maggie?"

"She's not going to be here for this meeting," Maeve says. "And, yes, it'll piss her right off, but it's the way it needs to be."

"We're hiring a private detective to do some research into Joey. After what Maggie told me the other day, we need answers. More than she'll be able to find by poking through his internet search history," Shawn says.

"I don't even know what an internet search history is," Kane says, shaking his head.

"Well, clearly, you can't be the one to investigate," I say, sidling up next to him. "And if you'd like me to leave so you can conduct your family business, I'm happy to do that."

"You'll stay," Kane says, his voice firm. The others nod. "I'd like your point of view on this. You're an unbiased third party."

"Well, third party is close enough," I say. "Where do we start?"

"With the most important piece," Keegan says. "We start at the money."

"You won't start anywhere."

CHAPTER FOURTEEN

~KANE~

We turn collectively at Maggie's voice, surprised that she's standing in the doorway of the kitchen.

"Are you psychic, then?" Shawn asks her with a half-smile.

"Something told me to come over," she says and shrugs. "And I know you're all trying to help, but it's not needed."

"You said yourself the other day that you need to know everything so you can let it go," I remind her. "This is the easiest way to do that."

"I was wrong." It's a whisper. She snatches Maeve's coffee and takes a long sip, then scowls at our sister. "It's not sweet enough."

"It's *my* coffee," Maeve reminds her. "And don't change the subject."

"I was able to finally get some answers yesterday

from one of the banks that's holding a lot of money," she says. "The beneficiary on the account is a Constance Lemon."

I frown, wracking my brain for family members of Joey's with that name, but I can't come up with any.

"Who's that?" Anastasia asks.

"Well, I didn't recognize the name," Maggie says, "and I know all of Joey's family. So I did a search. It turns out Constance is five years old."

"Minors can't be beneficiaries," Keegan says.

"Constance is the second name, the first is a Heather Fisher. Heather is Constance's mother. I'll give you one guess who her father is."

"Fucking hell," Shawn growls. "He had a *child*?"

"He did," Maggie confirms. "And as far as I'm concerned, they can have all of his money. I don't fucking care. I need to be done with this now, not after I've learned everything. Because each new thing is a fresh cut, and I don't deserve that."

"No, you don't," I agree and wrap my arm around her shoulders.

"I worry that this Heather and her child might try and sue the family," Maeve says, tapping her nail on her coffee mug. "If Constance truly is his daughter, Heather could attempt to get more than what's in those accounts."

"We'll cross that bridge if and when we come to it," Maggie says. "But for now, I need to move on. I know it's only been a few weeks, but with everything I've learned, I can't continue wallowing and worrying about someone who clearly didn't love me. It's a waste of time. So, I brought something."

She leaves the room and comes back, carrying a box.

"Are you moving in?" I ask her.

"No. But I've put the house on the market and might be looking for a place soon. This is Joey's computer, his phone, his briefcase, and wallet. Some other odds and ends. I can't throw it away because it's early, and what if someone needs something? But I can't have it near me because it's too tempting to keep looking through stuff. I need you to hide it from me, but keep it just in case."

"I can do that." I take the box and set it out in the sunroom for now. I know just where I'll put it. When I come back to the kitchen, Anastasia is in the pantry, rooting around.

"I can make muffins and bacon and eggs if anyone wants some breakfast," she calls out.

"I like her," Shawn says to me. "Hell, yes, we want some breakfast."

"Oh, Kane has champagne in here," Anastasia says with a triumphant hop as she walks back into the kitchen. "Mimosas, anyone?"

"You can stay," Maeve says, then looks at me. "She's staying."

"If I have anything to say about it, aye." My eyes are on the woman I love as she readies pots and pans, pulls ingredients out of the fridge, and sets the oven to preheat. "And not just because of her cooking skills."

"I saw her in the T-shirt," Keegan says and then starts to laugh when I glare at him. "You know I have to jab at you about that. Probably until the day you die."

"You'll be the first to die if you keep talking like that."

"Do they threaten each other with death often?" Anastasia asks.

"Daily," Maggie says. "They don't mean it. And, what did I miss?"

"I'll tell you about it later. It might have been the most embarrassing moment of my life," Anastasia says.

"Oh, this'll be good."

"What in the bleeding hell do you think you're doing?"

I'm glaring, ready to punch the kid who's fucking with my glass.

"I'm doing what Debbie asked me to, sir."

"Well, I know Debbie isn't stupid enough to tell you to put that there, so I'm going to advise you to stop right now and get the hell out of here."

"Yes, sir."

He marches out of the room as quickly as his overgrown feet can carry him, and I rub the back of my neck as I stare at the space around me.

The exhibit should be set up by now. I busted my ass to have the pieces finished and delivered to the museum three days ago.

"You really have to stop scaring my help." Debbie walks into the room, her heels clicking on the floor. "I thought I was going to have to give him a sedative."

"He was putting the red piece *here*." I point to the corner and watch as she deflates in defeat.

"Okay, fair enough. I'll go over the sketches with the help again."

"Feck it, I'll put it together myself."

"Kane, you're the artist. You don't have to do that."

"But I don't trust anyone else to do it, Debbie. This is the most important exhibit of my life, and it'll be done right."

She tips her head to the side, watching me with curiosity written all over her face. "All of your work is important."

"Not like this," I mutter and move the red piece to the side, then slip the purple where it's supposed to go. "Pass me that cart."

"Do you want to tell me *why* this one is more important than the others?"

"No." I carefully move the centerpiece, the most important part, onto the cart. It's too heavy for me to move across the room alone.

"This new work is more sensual than you've done before," Debbie says, walking slowly back and forth, taking it all in. "The twisty lines, the way it looks like that piece there is a couple intertwined with each other."

It's because this room is *us*, Anastasia and me. From the greens and blues of our time on the beach to the red-hot heat of intimacy. The colors bleed into each other, the pieces lock together.

It's Anastasia.

And I need it to be perfect because she'll be the first to see it finished.

"I've decided to add a couple of pieces," I inform Debbie, who only scowls at me. "You'll have them before the weekend since I'm heading out of town for a couple of days."

"I have the invitations ready to go for the showing," she says, checking something off on her iPad.

"There won't be a showing."

"Of course, there will be," she says. "Kane, we don't open up a new exhibit, a whole new *wing* of the museum, and not have a showing."

"Then you'll put it on hold," I insist and turn to her. "I won't be rushed in this, and it'll be done the way I say. I know you're the curator here, and I respect you, but this one is different, damn it."

"Okay." She holds up a hand in surrender. "It's good I haven't sent the invites out yet, then. Let me know when I can move forward with it."

"I will. And in the meantime, *no one* comes in here but you or me. And I mean it, Debbie. If early photos get leaked, if *anything* happens to any of these pieces, it'll be your ass."

"Top secret." She nods once and makes another note. "Got it. You've always been a mysterious man, Kane. Why change now?"

"I'll set the rest of these and then I'll be gone for the day," I inform her. "But I'll be back in the morning."

"Sounds good to me. I'll bring in some breakfast." She walks out, leaving me alone in the room.

The seascape room, the one where I first met Anastasia, has always been my favorite. It reminds me of the dangerous and choppy sea of Ireland. My mind was there while I worked on the pieces, and the final result mirrored that vision perfectly. It's where I go to think of home, and when I need a moment to remember why I work my fingers to the bone.

Yes, glass is in my soul, and I'll work with sand and fire until the day I die. But I've never had a need to share the results of my labor with anyone else. If it weren't for my agent, and the interest of some important people, this museum likely wouldn't exist. I'd be content keeping it all for myself.

But the day I found Anastasia sitting on that bench, working feverishly with pen and paper, and she admitted to me that my art inspires hers…I was reminded that work fuels work, and art feeds art.

The work on display here has given my family a life none of us ever dreamed of. And it's given me an outlet to share what I love most.

Soon, that will include Anastasia, although only she and I will understand that.

Once I'm satisfied that the pieces on hand are just the way they should be, I leave the museum for the day, waving at Debbie in her office as I walk out the back door to my car.

I have a date with a beautiful woman.

The drive to Anastasia's place takes a while from Tacoma through the traffic. Still, when I park and walk into her bakery, it's totally worth it when she smiles and hurries over to give me a kiss.

"How has your day been?" she asks, reaching behind me to flip the lock on the door.

"Busy. But it's suddenly much better."

"Same." She kisses my chin and then walks behind the counter. "I decorated two cakes today, and it was glorious."

"I hope you didn't lift them."

"No, Rebecca just left for the day. She's been working extra hours this week, so she's here to move the cakes for me. Being able to at least decorate them has been awesome, though. I'm a little tired, but my shoulder feels pretty good."

"Just don't get over-confident and hurt yourself again." I lean over to kiss her nose. "Are you hungry?"

"Starving. Where are we going?"

"I seem to remember you saying you've been in the mood for a burger, so we'll go to Red Mill."

"Holy shit, now I'm hungrier." She laughs, tidies the

desk, and once she's locked up and turned off the lights, I lead her to my car.

The drive back across the Seattle metro area isn't fast, but now that I have her with me, holding my hand, I don't mind the traffic so much.

"There's not even a line out the door," she says with excitement as we approach the building. "That's unusual."

"Is it that good?"

"You've never been? Oh, you're in for a treat. Yes, it's that good. Come on."

We order our burgers with bacon and all the fixings, fries and drinks, and then find a table in the tiny dining room.

"Not a lot of space in here," I say.

"When the weather's nice, a lot of people sit outside. Or wait for a table."

It doesn't take long for my name to be called, and when I take my first bite of burger, I close my eyes in delight.

"Told you," Anastasia says. "Best ever."

"I've had burgers all over the world, and this is the best one I've had."

She smiles smugly and pops a French fry into her mouth. I can't talk because I'm too busy stuffing my face. I didn't realize I was so hungry.

"Well, fancy meeting you here."

"Hey!" Anastasia stands and hugs Meg, then Will, who's eyeing Anastasia's fries. "Don't touch."

"I've got my own fries coming," Will says with a laugh. "Small world."

"Kane's never been here," Anastasia says.

"It's the best," Meg says. "And it's where I met Will for the first time."

"Really?" I'm intrigued. "Of all of the places to meet, this was it?"

"Well, he loves food," Meg reminds me. "And he was here with Jules, who was a college friend of mine. I came to say hello and met him in the process."

"She hated me." Will smiles widely, enjoying the story. "Like, *hated* me."

"She doesn't now," Anastasia says. "Do you guys want to join us?"

"Thanks, but no. We have to get back to the girls. We just came to get dinner to go."

"The girls don't eat burgers?" I ask.

"Well, Erin's two, so all she wants is chicken strips, and she has a fondness for chips and salsa," Will replies. "And Zoey's only one, so her palate hasn't expanded to burgers yet."

"Enjoy your dinner," Meg says with a wave when her name is called, and they hurry out, carrying a massive brown bag full of hot food.

"I like them." I take a bite of my burger and chew thoughtfully. "I like all of your family."

"I'm glad. I like yours, too."

"It's helpful, don't you think?"

"To like each other's families?" She nods and takes a

sip of her milkshake. "Absolutely. When you're with someone, you're sort of with their loved ones, too. So, if you couldn't stand my family, this probably would be a no-go for me. And vice versa."

I nod in agreement. "Come home with me tonight."

"I can't."

I raise a brow. "Why not?"

"Because I'm going over to Maggie's."

I blink at her, making her laugh.

"We're having a girls' night out tonight. I invited Joy and Amelia, and Maggie and Maeve are coming. Maggie needs to let off some steam."

"You're going out partying?"

"At the pub," she says with a shrug as if it's nothing. "And, no, you're not invited. No boys allowed."

"It's my family's bloody pub. Who's to stop me from coming to have a beer with Shawn?"

"Me." She pops another fry into her mouth. "I'm stopping you. Let your sister have some fun tonight. We'll keep an eye on her. And then we'll probably crash at her house."

"You can come to *my* house when you're done."

I've come to think of it as *our* house, but I don't know that either of us is ready for me to admit that yet.

"I'll come over in the morning," she promises.

"I have to be at the museum in the morning."

"Oh, that's unusual."

"We're putting the new exhibit together, and I don't

trust the clumsy idiots Debbie's hired to move pieces around."

"Is Debbie the woman I saw the day I met you?"

I nod. "She's the curator for the museum. And I trust her, but I want to have more of a hands-on approach with this one. I'll probably leave home around eight."

"I'll make sure I see you before you leave," she promises. "Don't pout."

"I do not pout."

"You're totally pouting." She laughs and offers me the last of her fries. "It's only one night, Kane."

"It's one night too many." But I resign myself to being alone this evening. "I'd like to take you away this weekend."

"I've only just been able to get back to work, and I have some things to—" She stops talking and looks at me, then takes a deep breath. "This is important to you."

"It is, aye."

"When should I be ready?"

I reach over for her hand. "Friday morning."

"Where are we going?"

"That's a surprise, *mo ghrá*."

CHAPTER FIFTEEN

~ANASTASIA~

"She sings like an angel."

We're sitting in a corner booth, sipping lemon drop martinis. Maggie's singing with the small band as Lia, Joy, Maeve, and I look on.

The music isn't sad this time. It's fast and lively, and several of the regulars are dancing a jig on the floor.

I never thought I'd see the day that I'd see someone dance a jig, but...here we are.

"I can't move like that," Lia says, gesturing to the woman dancing beautifully with her arms straight at her side. "It's amazing."

"Maggie and I took lessons when we were young," Maeve says with a smile. "Music was always important in our family, and truth be told, our culture. So, we sing and dance, and Kane even learned to play the fiddle when he was a lad in Ireland."

"Really?" I stare at Maeve in shock. "He never told me he can play."

"I'd say there's probably a lot of things about each other you're still learning," Joy says. "How's your shoulder feeling?"

"Tons better. And no, I'm not overdoing it."

"Good."

Maggie finishes her song and hurries over to us, then drinks what's left of her martini. "I've never had this drink before. I usually just drink beer. This is fancy."

"It's vodka and lemonade," Lia says and laughs. "But the lemon peel makes it look fancy."

"Keegan's good at making drinks," Maggie says, giving her brother a proud smile from across the room. "I wonder where Kane and Shawn are?"

"They're not allowed in here tonight," Maeve replies. "We're here to let off some steam, and we'll do it without being judged by our brothers."

"Why does Keegan get to be here?" I ask.

"Because there are no drinks without him," Maeve says.

"We could have gone somewhere in the city," Joy suggests. "Where no one can judge."

"I'd like to stay close to home for now," Maggie admits. "I know it seems silly, but it feels safest. I've been keeping a low profile."

"Here, have another drink," I suggest, pushing my untouched lemon drop to Maggie. "You need it."

"You've no idea how right you are," Maggie says. "Is it wrong that I've been drunk more since Joey died than I ever was when he was alive?"

"No. The man would drive anyone to drink," Maeve says. "And we're not here to talk about him."

"Oh, Stasia," Joy says in excitement. "My sister asked me to ask you if you would be willing to make her wedding cake."

"Of course! When is Noel getting married?"

"In a few months. But we know you book up quickly. She and Reed will come see you."

"That's lovely," Maggie says with a wistful sigh.

"Mary Margaret, you need more liquor," Maeve says, signaling to Keegan for another round.

"Let's talk about sex," Lia suggests and giggles. She's had a few lemon drops of her own, and her cheeks are nice and rosy. "That's what girls' night out is for, right?"

"I mean, I'm not getting any," Maeve says with a frown. "And it's a damn shame."

"I don't want any," Maggie adds. "Never again."

"*Never* again?" I ask, shocked. "I mean, it makes sense that you're not ready right now, but you're only, what? Twenty-four?"

"Twenty-five," she says. "Maybe I should just join a convent. Dedicate myself to God for all of time."

"That would be a shame. No offense," Lia says. "I'm sure that for some, that's the right path. But you're just sad. And mad. And you totally should be."

As soon as we arrived at the pub, and before we could get many drinks into her, Maggie told Joy and Lia all about finding out about Joey's affairs and the child that was the result of one of them.

"But don't give up on men altogether," Joy adds. "There are some good ones out there. You just found a lemon."

Maggie snorts. "That was his last name. And my siblings got a huge kick out of it, always calling him a lemon. Because he was."

"But not all men are," I repeat. "And there are some who will not only be nice to you but also give you the most amazing orgasms you've ever had in your life."

"I've never had an orgasm," Maggie admits, slurring her words just a bit.

We all sit in shocked silence.

"Well, that's a damn shame," Lia finally says.

"And it should be illegal," I agree.

"Maybe there's a hot man here tonight who could give me an orgasm," Maggie says, scanning the room.

"All I see is a bunch of old guys who don't want to go home to their wives, so they're sitting here getting drunk," Maeve says. "You know, the usual."

"Wait." Joy points to a guy at the end of the bar, chatting with Keegan. "Who's that?"

"Oh, that's just Cameron," Maggie says, shaking her head. "Trust me, he's not orgasm material."

As if he can hear our conversation, Cameron glances our way.

"I don't know," Lia says, shaking her head. "He's pretty hot. Why isn't he in the running?"

"Because he's Kane's best friend," I say, guessing. "And he's more like a brother?"

"Well, he's Kane's bestie, but I wouldn't call him a brother," Maggie says with a frown. "By the time I was old enough to find Cameron attractive, he was off with the military. I don't know him that well."

"Then why isn't he in the running?" Joy asks again. "Because did you see his arms? Good God, those biceps are ridiculous."

"Uh, ladies, he looks suspicious," I say and laugh, watching as Cameron narrows his eyes at us, clearly suspecting that something's up. "Staring at him while we talk isn't exactly incognito."

"He's not the one to give me orgasms," Maggie says again, shaking her head woefully. "He doesn't stick around for long."

"All the better," Lia says with a grin. "You can take him for a test drive, and then when he leaves, there's no harm, no foul."

"You have a point."

"I don't think we were striving for orgasms tonight," I say, trying to be the voice of reason.

"I'm totally getting some," Joy says and pulls her phone out of her pocket. "In fact, I'm gonna text Jace right now and give him a heads-up."

"Oh, fun," Lia says, reaching for her cell. "I'll do the same."

She holds the phone out and puckers her lips, snaps the photo, and sends it on to her husband.

"Now that you mention it," Maggie says, still eyeing poor Cameron. "He is hot. Maybe all I need is a one-night stand to work off some of this aggression."

"He looks like he could give you some amazing, rough sex," Joy says.

"Maeve hasn't said anything," I point out, watching the other woman as she nibbles on her lip.

"Do *you* have a crush on Cameron, Maeve?" Maggie asks her sister.

"No. Definitely not. I'm trying to be Switzerland over here. You're a grown woman. I have no opinion."

"That's no fun," I say.

"It's all you're going to get from me," Maeve says.

"I'm gonna go talk to him," Maggie says and sucks down the rest of her drink. She slides from the booth, flips her hair over her shoulder, and walks across the bar to where Cameron's sitting.

We watch in fascination as Cameron turns to Maggie and smiles. She says something, and his expression turns from friendly to hot lust in about a millisecond.

"Oh, he's interested," Lia says. "Did you see how his entire body just went on red-alert?"

"Damn hot," Joy mutters. "Holy shit."

He shakes his head, and Maggie laughs, resting her hand on Cameron's shoulder.

And then, to our utter shock, he takes her hand,

kisses it, and then stands and walks her right out of the bar.

"Uh, guys? Maggie just left with a dude." I stare at the empty seat where Cameron was just sipping his beer. The glass still mostly full.

"With *Cameron*," Maeve whispers, just as shocked as I am.

"Well, then." Lia swallows. "Looks like Maggie might get that orgasm, after all."

"Wow," Joy says. "You guys, I'm *so* impressed. It takes balls of steel to do what she just did."

Suddenly, Jace and Wyatt come walking into the bar and head straight for our table.

"I didn't know you guys were coming," I say.

"We came to collect our women," Wyatt says with a soft smile for Lia. "We figured they'd be good and buzzed by now."

"I'm super buzzed," Joy agrees. "And I'm ready for some orgasms."

Jace's eyebrows climb into his hairline in surprise. "Well, that sounds like a good plan."

Lia and Joy wave at Maeve and me and then follow their men out of the bar.

"It's just you and me," Maeve says on a sigh.

"What's your story?" I ask, realizing that I don't know much about Maeve. "No guy in your life?"

"Not in a long time," she says. "I'm busy with work and with this big family of mine. In case you haven't noticed, they're a lot."

"I get it." I clink my glass to hers. "Family can be demanding. I have a big, needy family of my own."

"But I love them." She sighs. "I think I'll head home and call it a day. Do you need a ride to Kane's?"

"She doesn't."

My head whirls at the sound of Kane's voice.

"I didn't even see you there."

"I'll see you both later."

Maeve leaves, and Kane kisses my hand. "Where did everyone go?"

"Wyatt and Jace came to pick up the girls. Maggie left with someone."

Those amazing green eyes whip to mine. "What did you just say?"

"Don't freak out. She's safe."

"Who?"

"I shouldn't tell you."

"You'd bloody well better tell me."

"She hit on Cameron. And they left together."

Kane's jaw drops. He blinks rapidly and then shakes his head.

"Let's go home."

"You're not mad?"

"I don't know what I am. At the end of the day, she's an adult, and it's none of my business."

He licks his lips, shuffles his feet, and then mutters *"bollocks"* as he takes his phone out of his pocket and taps on the screen.

"You're carrying your phone."

"And it's a damn good thing I am so I can text Cameron and tell him not to act the maggot or I'll kill him. I don't care how skilled he is."

"So, we're taking a road trip," I guess as Kane steers his beautiful Porsche onto the freeway, headed away from the airport.

"Yes," he confirms and glances in the side mirror before changing lanes. "We've about a four-hour drive ahead of us, but there's no better way to get there."

"I like road trips," I reply, settling into the buttery-soft leather seat. "After Lia was able to finalize her divorce and close up her life in LA, I flew down and drove back to Seattle with her. The moving truck was a few days ahead of us, but we had all of her valuables in her SUV, and it only took us two days to make it back to Seattle."

"I didn't realize she was married before Wyatt."

"Yeah, she was married to a massive douchebag. He was such an ass. Controlling. Mean. Mocked her career choice, even after it started bringing in a lot of money, and she started seeing some success."

"It sounds like he was jealous," Kane says, disgust heavy in his voice.

"Oh, for sure. He just couldn't deal. Lia kept a lot of what happened to herself, mostly because she didn't want to burden the rest of us. And I think also because, when you're married, you feel like you have to take your spouse's side. Because of that, she withdrew from us when she was married to that asshole."

I watch out the passenger window as the city fades and we're surrounded by more trees, more wilderness.

"So, let's just say no love was lost when she finally left him. It was a messy divorce. Then he contested it, so even though she'd been legally divorced, they reversed it, and she had to go through more mediation and court."

"That sounds horrifying," he says.

"It was awful. She met Wyatt, and they fell in love. But when he discovered that she wasn't legally divorced, he lost his shit. It was horrible for both of them."

"But they came out the other side of it just fine."

"They did." I nod, and we grow quiet as Kane drives us on the freeway, headed toward Portland.

I raise a brow when he takes the exit headed toward the ocean beaches, then ventures off the main freeway and onto a smaller highway.

"I enjoy the beach."

His lips twitch in humor. "As do I. Have you been to the coast of Oregon?"

"A couple of times when we were young," I confirm. "But it's been a long time."

"I found an amazing hotel in Cannon Beach," Kane says. "You're going to love it."

DREAM WITH ME

He's not wrong.

The Stephanie Inn is breathtaking. At only three stories tall, I would consider it a boutique hotel, nestled between the coastline mountains and the rolling waves of the Pacific. The lobby features a tall, rock fireplace, and a table is set up all day with fresh muffins, scones, and coffee.

We're welcomed and escorted to our room on the third floor. The first thing I do is hurry to the ocean-view deck, open the door, and step out onto the spacious balcony.

Once the bellman has delivered the bags, and Kane bids him farewell, Kane joins me, wraps his arms around me from behind, and buries his lips against my neck.

"This is incredible."

"Told you."

I smile and watch as couples walk on the sand, hand in hand toward the enormous rock down the beach.

"That's Haystack Rock," Kane says, pointing. "We'll walk down later."

"Murphy would love this."

"Unfortunately, the hotel doesn't allow pets."

"Hmm. Shame." I turn in his arms and hug him close. "Thank you for this."

"Thank you for joining me." He kisses the top of my head. "I thought we could use a couple of days away.

Since I met you, it's been one thing after another with my family, and your injury. I wanted some time to just enjoy you. Learn you."

I smile and take a deep breath, enjoying the combination of Kane's cologne and the sea air.

"That's a great idea. Maybe the best idea you've ever had."

"Look."

I turn and look where he's pointing, out into the ocean. Water sprays up into the air, and I gasp in delight.

"Whales!"

"It's a good time of year to see them," he says. "We don't get many where we are up amidst the islands. We should get to see our share while we're here."

"I already feel relaxed," I admit. "And not in the lazy way I was when I was recovering from my shoulder."

"That wasn't relaxing," he says with a frown. "That was healing. There's a difference."

"You're right."

He checks the time. "It's about six. Are you hungry?"

"Starving."

I change into fresh clothes, brush my hair, and swipe on a fresh coat of mascara, then consider that good enough.

Lia would be mortified that I don't have a full face on, but I've never been the makeup lover that my sister is.

When I walk out of the massive bathroom that

happens to boast a separate tub and a walk-in shower, double sinks, and a vanity area—all bigger than the master bathroom in my apartment—I see that Kane's also changed into a pair of khaki slacks and a blue button-down shirt.

"You look nice. Are we going out somewhere fancy? Should I change?"

I glance down at my simple black skinny jeans and green V-neck sweater.

"No, you look amazing. We're just going downstairs."

He takes my hand and leads me down to the library, just off the foyer, where the hotel has set up a wine tasting with a cheese and cracker spread that looks beautiful *and* delicious.

"Welcome," the employee manning the wine says. She tells us about the six local Oregon wines they're offering tonight, pours us each a glass, and then invites us to come eat and enjoy the sunset from the comfort of cozy chairs by the fire.

"This could become addicting," I confess as I settle in with a plate of food and my wine. "Do they do this all the time, or is it a special occasion?"

"This is an everyday thing," Kane confirms. "Don't get too full. We're headed to dinner after this."

"There's *more*?" I sip my sweet white wine and watch the sun kiss the water beyond the windows of the inn, enjoying this quiet time with Kane. "I feel spoiled."

"It's spoiled you should feel every day of your life, my sweet," Kane says, kicking up his accent just a bit for my benefit.

Once the sun has sunk all the way into the water, and my belly is halfway to full, we make our way up one floor to the small dining room.

This hotel may be off the beaten path, but everything about it is absolute luxury. The linens on the table are soft, and the lighting is romantic.

"We'll be down here each morning for breakfast, as well," Kane informs me after we're seated. "It might be one of the best restaurants I've been to in my life."

"I can't believe I've never heard of this place," I admit. "It's *amazing*."

"Best kept secret that's not so much a secret on the west coast," the waiter says as he joins us. "And I'm happy to hear you're pleased with your stay so far, Miss Montgomery."

"Thank you."

I'm not even going to try and guess how he knows my name. So far, every staff member has greeted us by name since we checked in.

It's like everyone's psychic.

The menu is the same for everyone. Tonight, they're serving fresh Dungeness crab that was caught this afternoon from the ocean right outside, along with an array of sides that have my mouth watering.

"I shouldn't have had the cheese and crackers," I mutter, staring at the food before me.

"There's no rush," Kane assures me. "We can take our time and enjoy."

"It's going to take me all evening to eat this," I admit. "And I *am* eating every bite. It's too good not to."

He smiles and takes a bite of the fresh, hot bread just delivered to our table.

"I do enjoy watching you eat your food, Anastasia."

"Well, then, I'm about to put on one hell of a show."

CHAPTER SIXTEEN

~ANASTASIA~

My feet are killing me.

We walked for miles on the beach this morning. Then, we took the inn's shuttle to downtown Cannon Beach, where we've walked all over town, in and out of some of the most beautiful art galleries I've ever seen. Paintings, sculptures, you name it can be found in this gem of a town.

If I didn't have a business and family in Seattle, I'd move here right now. Open up a little cake shop and live the rest of my days walking the beach and making delicious cakes for the sweet people we've met here.

"Where are you, darling?"

I smile at Kane. We're walking between galleries, just enjoying a leisurely stroll. "Daydreaming."

"And what would that daydream be?"

I laugh and shake my head. "Nothing. It's silly."

Something in a window catches my eye. "Oh, let's go in here."

Kane follows me into the building. It's quiet in here today. It's so pretty outside, most of the tourists are likely on the beach, enjoying the water and the sunshine.

"I love this." I walk over to a bronze sculpture of a girl, maybe in her early teens. Her hair is up in a ponytail, and she's holding a paintbrush, leaning in with squinting eyes, looking at a canvas.

The art she's painting is also part of the sculpture, and absolutely stunning.

"Oh, how lovely," I breathe. "Look at the detail, all the way down to her toenails."

"You have good taste."

Kane and I turn at the sound of the voice. A man in his mid-thirties smiles at us and nods at the piece I'm admiring.

"This artist lives south of here. I've sold her pieces for years."

"I can see why," I reply. "She does beautiful work."

"You're Kane O'Callaghan." He holds his hand out for Kane to shake. "I'm Trevor Mullins, the owner of this gallery, and several more all over the world."

"I've heard your name," Kane says as he shakes Trevor's hand. "It's a pleasure to meet you."

"The pleasure's all mine," Trevor says with a smile.

"I'm going to let you two talk while I look around." I

nod politely. "I see several pieces that have caught my eye."

I walk away and let Trevor try to impress Kane enough to sell some of his pieces here in the gallery. I think Kane should do it. I can see by looking around that Trevor has a discerning eye, with only the best work on display.

Frankly, I could go into deep, deep debt by shopping in here, with that sculpture of the girl painting at the top of my list. There's also a seascape that I can't stop looking at. The colors are muted, subdued greens and blues that perfectly portray a moody ocean.

It would be a gorgeous piece for Kane's master bedroom. It reminds me of Kane. Subdued and a little moody, but magnificent and powerful.

I check the price, convinced I need to buy it for Kane's birthday, and am surprised to see it's only a couple thousand dollars. I discreetly tuck Trevor's card into my pocket and make a mental note to call him when I'm back home to make arrangements to purchase the painting and have it delivered to me in Seattle.

When I walk back to the men, Kane's shaking Trevor's hand.

"I'll be in touch, then," Kane says with a nod and wraps his arm around my shoulders. "Are you ready, darling?"

"I am. Have a good day."

"Enjoy your stay in our little town." Trevor waves as

we turn to leave. Once we're on the sidewalk, I face Kane.

"Can I be brutally honest?"

"Always, you know that."

"My feet are *killing me*."

His lips twitch, and he kisses my forehead. "It's no wonder, we've been walking all day. I'll call the shuttle."

Ten minutes later, the driver arrives. It's given us enough time to find a latte to take back to the inn with us.

On our way through the lobby to the elevator, I can't help but make a stop at the goody station and snatch a cranberry orange scone for a snack.

"Take two," Kane urges me. "I'll join you."

Armed with our coffees and scones, we set off for our room. While we were gone, housekeeping came in to make the bed and leave fresh towels.

There's a brown teddy bear in our room, and the housekeeper arranged it on the bed with the remote control in his hands as if he's watching TV.

"That's adorable."

I kick off my shoes, quickly change into some yoga pants, and walk out to the balcony.

"These cushioned chaise lounges are *so* comfy," I inform Kane as he joins me.

"And wide enough for two. Convenient."

"Mm." I sip my coffee and watch the waves for a moment. "This is a nice break."

"I'm glad you suggested we take it easy this afternoon. We're here to relax, and if this is how you want to do that, I'm all for it."

I kiss his cheek and lean against his shoulder. "You know, Maeve reminded me the other night that you and I still have a lot to learn about each other."

"Did she now?" He kisses my temple. "She's probably right. What would you like to know?"

"Well, first of all, when is your birthday?"

"December the twelfth."

Good. I didn't miss it. My birthday plans for that painting are perfect.

"And yours?" he asks me.

"October tenth."

He pulls away to stare down at me.

"What?"

"That's next week."

I nod and take a bite of my scone. "I seriously need to get the recipe for these. I wonder if the baker would give it to me?"

"You've changed the subject."

"I thought we'd finished the other subject."

"Were you going to tell me that your birthday is *next week*?"

"It probably would have come up in conversation."

He quietly chews a bite of his scone.

"I should take you over my knee, Anastasia."

I laugh, then kiss his chin. "Don't change the subject."

"Your eyes are the same color as the ocean right

now," he murmurs, his voice lazy and calm. "I noticed at the barbeque with your family that many of you have the same eyes."

"We do. Your family all has green eyes."

"Aye," he says with a nod.

"Why did your parents move to Seattle?"

He sips his coffee, watching the water. "Da said it was for more opportunity. The village we're from is outside of Galway, and it's small. Poor. Mostly comprised of farmers. Da wasn't a good farmer. But he was an excellent pub owner."

"And he didn't want to own a pub in Ireland?"

"He wanted us to have more options," Kane says, choosing his words carefully. "Education, experiences. He'd read an article about Seattle, and loved the photos featured, so he and Mum packed us up and moved."

"Because of an *article*? He'd never been before?"

"There wasn't enough money to send him out on a scouting mission. No, we all just packed up and came. Shawn was only two, and Maggie hadn't been born yet. Da wanted us to be closer to the water, so he bought the building the pub's in. We lived upstairs for a year until they saved enough to buy a house. Maggie was born upstairs."

"That's incredible." I have the best view of the ocean a person could ask for, but I can't stop watching Kane, and the love on his face as he speaks about his family. "You must be so proud of them."

"I was angry," he confesses. "I didn't want to come

to America. I wanted to stay with my grandparents, learn the fiddle, raise horses, and learn to make glass with my uncle. I loved our life in Ireland. But I was only twelve when we moved and didn't understand that they were doing what they thought was best for our family, not leaving because they wanted to take us away from everything else."

"Are your grandparents still alive?" I ask.

"They are." He smiles. "And healthy as can be. You'll meet them."

"You said you go to Ireland every year?"

"Aye, for two months in the summer. It's the best time to be there. But I enjoy the winter, too. It reminds me a lot of Washington, with rainy weather and cool days."

"What do you miss the most?"

His green eyes soften. "'Tis a magical land, Ireland. You'll hear stories of faeries and ghosts. Legends. All true, of course. When you walk those green hills, sprinkled with bluebells and columbine, and wander among ruins of castles that have been there for a thousand years or more, you can't help but feel the magic of it. It sinks into your soul, it does, and it's an ache that sits within you until you're able to go back again."

The sorrow in his words brings tears to my eyes. "You love it."

"Very much."

I lean my head on his shoulder again and watch the

DREAM WITH ME

waves crash on the wet sand below us. Kane kisses my head, and we sit in silence.

"What were you daydreaming about earlier?" he asks quietly.

"Living here," I confess on a heavy sigh. "I thought that if I didn't have my business and family in Seattle, I'd pack right up and move here. Sell cakes in that adorable little town, and live on the water."

"It's a lovely place," he says. "It's glad I am that you're enjoying it."

"Very much." I set my empty latte cup aside and turn to snuggle him. "This is my new favorite place."

"We'll come often, then." He kisses my nose. "As often as you like."

"I'm a spoiled woman."

"Treasured," he corrects me. "And it's as it should be."

"Oh, God, yes."

I clap my hands in excitement the next morning. After we took our time waking up and wandered down for a delicious breakfast, Kane informed me that we're about to get a couple's massage.

"I haven't had a massage in months. I need it."

"It'll probably feel good on your shoulder," Kane says as someone knocks on the door.

"They're coming *here*?"

"Of course." He opens the door and frowns when a man and a woman walk into the room, both carrying tables and supplies.

"Good morning, Mr. O'Callaghan," the woman says. "I'm Nell, and this is Charlie. We'll be your therapists today."

"We can do this a couple of ways," Charlie continues and turns to me. "Miss, do you prefer a man or a woman therapist?"

"Um, well—"

"Both of you can go," Kane says, shocking the hell out of me.

"What?"

"I've changed my mind." Kane shakes his head. "But please leave one of the tables and the oil."

"Sir, I don't think—" Nell begins, but Charlie holds a hand up, stopping her.

"We were told to do whatever you wish, so that's fine. I'll set the table up for you, and you can just call down when you're finished, and I'll come back to collect it."

Charlie and Nell quickly set up the table, drape linens on top, and set oil on a side table. When they've left, Kane turns to me.

"What in the world has gotten into you?" I ask.

"There was no way in hell that man was going to put his hands on you," he says, walking slowly toward me. "And call me stupid, but I'm not a fan of a man rubbing me down, either."

"So you just kicked him out?"

"Yes." His green eyes are steady on mine, and when he reaches me, he pulls the belt of my robe loose and lets it drop to the floor. The robe parts, exposing my naked flesh beneath it. "Get on the table, Anastasia."

"*You're* going to massage me?"

"I am." He peels the robe down my arms and watches boldly as I pull back the sheet and lay on the table, my face in the cradle.

I take a deep breath and smile to myself when I hear the gas fireplace coming to life.

"I don't want you to get cold." Kane exposes my back, down to the top of my ass, and then his hands are on me, strong and sure, gliding up and down my back in long, firm strokes.

"Oh, man, that feels good. Have I told you that I love your hands?"

"I don't think you have, no. But my hands are rough. I probably shouldn't be doing this to you."

"They feel good," I assure him. "That feels especially wonderful on my low back."

He hangs out there, kneading the muscles firmly, and I'm pretty sure I'm either going to fall asleep or have an orgasm, it feels so damn good.

And just when I think it can't get better, he moves up to my neck and shoulders. Kane is gentle around my injured shoulder, careful not to move it too much. Still, the light kneading around my shoulder blade and neck on that side feels absolutely *amazing*.

"No other man gets to hear you make that noise," he says casually.

"What noise?"

"Those light moans. Sighs." His hand glides down my spine, and I let out a long breath. "That. Those sounds are mine."

He pushes the sheet farther down my ass, exposing more of my flesh, and starts to knead my glutes.

"He doesn't get to see this, how the goose flesh appears on your skin when I touch you. Or these dimples here, just above this fantastic ass you have."

He rubs in circles, and then his fingers slide down the crease of my ass inward, barely skimming along the lips of my pussy. I'm immediately a hot ball of raw need.

"Kane."

"Aye, 'tis only me, Anastasia." He rubs my thighs down to my knees and up again, his fingers finding my core wetter now. "I feckin love your body's reaction to my touch."

"I love it when you touch me," I admit, my hips instinctively pushing back, wanting more. My nipples are painfully hard against the table, every nerve ending on high alert. I want more of him. I *need* him.

He slips two fingers inside me and rubs slowly in and out, his thumb gently grazing over my anus, making everything inside me clench.

"A more beautiful woman I've never seen, and that's the truth of it," he says and leans over to press his lips to my ear. "You drive me bleeding crazy. I want you every minute of every day. You make me mad with longing, and it's not just your body I'm wanting, but *everything*. Your happiness and your struggles. Your sassiness."

My breathing comes in hard gasps. I'm right there, right on the edge of coming apart, when he takes his fingers out and pulls me to the edge of the table so my legs hang off the side and he can enter me from behind.

We both moan in relief when he's balls-deep. Kane bites the ball of my good shoulder, and then begins a rough rhythm, in and out while still massaging my shoulders and then down to my breasts. His thumbs brush over my nipples, and I clench around him, already about to lose my grip on this orgasm.

"You're mine only, Anastasia Montgomery."

And that's all it takes to have me falling over the edge into lust and love and romance.

I barely have a chance to catch my breath before he slips out of me, turns me over, and slides right back in, his eyes locked on mine. He pulls my ankles up to rest on his shoulders as he cups my ass, gripping hard as he rides me until he bares his teeth and succumbs to his own climax.

He slips out of me, lifts me into his arms, and carries me into the bathroom.

"Give me one minute," he says as he sets me on my feet and opens the door to start the shower, letting the water get good and hot before he takes my hand and leads me under the spray.

He tugs me against him and nudges my chin up so he can kiss me soft and slow.

"I'm irreversibly and completely in love with you." His words are soft but steady. Sure. "Being with you is a special form of magic that I never want to lose."

"I love you, too." My fingers brush through the hair at the nape of his neck. "Completely and irreversibly."

His next kiss is possessive. Elated. Urgent. And here, in this gorgeous place, tucked in an opulent shower, we murmur words of love and promise to each other.

It's the most important moment of my life.

CHAPTER SEVENTEEN

~KANE~

I'm on my way to the pub for an evening of chatter with my brothers and sisters and a bowl of stew. Since Maggie's been working for Keegan more often, she's started making Mum's stew for the customers, and I must admit, she's damn good at it.

So, while Anastasia is at her house tonight, catching up on work, I'll spend some time with my siblings and ask their opinions on some things.

Just as I park my car, my phone rings, surprising me. I've been carrying the damn thing with me more, but I'm still not used to it.

"This is Kane."

"Hello, Kane, this is Trevor Mullins. I met you last week in Cannon Beach."

"Yes, I remember who you are, Trevor. What can I do for you?"

"Well, first of all, I have the sculpture you purchased

wrapped up, and I'll be driving it up to Seattle myself tomorrow. I have business up there in my Bellevue gallery, so this is convenient for both of us."

I grin, thinking of the piece of the girl painting, and the look on Anastasia's face when she first saw it. She had stars in her eyes, and I knew then and there that she'd have it. The fact that her birthday is in two days is absolutely wonderful timing.

"Perfect, thank you. I'll be out that way tomorrow and can meet up with you then."

"I'll text you when I'm in town. The other reason I was calling is a professional matter. Or, a proposal, if you will."

I narrow my eyes, intrigued. "Go on."

"I know you're a very busy man with the museum and private exhibits already on display all over the world, but I thought I'd give this a try anyway. I recently opened a gallery in Galway, Ireland, and I've decided to do something very different with it. I'd like to display works made specifically by Irish artists, similar to my Cannon Beach gallery. Only Oregon artists are on display there.

"After meeting you last week, I knew that I had to at least reach out to you to see if I could talk you into a show in Galway. Of course, the pieces would have to be exclusive, and I would take fifteen percent of every sale."

I chuckle. "Ten percent, and not a penny more, Trevor. But what's the timing on this?"

"I'm aiming for a Christmas show," he says. "I know it's not much time, but again, I needed to ask. You're one of the most prominent artists, and certainly the most highly acclaimed glass artist to come out of Ireland."

And having a showing in Galway, less than a hundred miles from where my family's from, would be a dream come true.

But I have responsibilities here, a new exhibit opening in my museum, my family, and if all goes as planned, a wedding to prepare for.

"I think I have to pass on that timing," I inform Trevor. "I appreciate the offer, and it's a tempting one to be sure, but Christmas isn't doable for me."

"Think it over," Trevor suggests. "And let me know if you change your mind. I'll see you tomorrow."

He hangs up, and I simply shake my head and walk inside. The evening crowd in O'Callaghan's Pub isn't as full tonight as it usually is. I wave at a group of older men in the corner, who've been coming into the pub for many years, and then sit at the bar.

"And look what the cat dragged in," Keegan says, wiping off the counter with a white towel. "What can we get for you, brother of mine?"

"Stew, and a pint."

"You like my stew," Maggie says with a smile as she loads up a tray with drinks to be delivered. She glances at me and then frowns. "What's wrong?"

"What? Oh, nothing." I shrug a shoulder, but Maggie's like a pit bull and won't let it go.

"Your face says something's wrong. Is Stasia okay?"

"She's fine."

"Maybe he doesn't want to talk about it," Shawn suggests, taking the stool next to me.

"I'm here, aren't I?" I scowl and then smile at Maeve, who delivers my stew. "It's a regular family affair in here tonight."

"What's wrong?" Maeve asks, making me scowl, but Maggie points at our sister in victory.

"See! Something's wrong."

"I just had a call with the offer of an exclusive gallery showing in Galway, but I passed on it."

My siblings are all quiet for a long moment, and then Shawn reaches over and smacks me on the back of the head.

"Hey!"

"Clearly, you have a screw loose," Shawn says.

"Why would you pass that up?" Maeve asks.

"Because they need brand new pieces by Christmas, and that's only two months away. I'm about to open an all new exhibit in the museum, and I have other responsibilities here."

"But you've always wanted an exhibit in Ireland," Keegan reminds me.

"And I can have one later. I've just not pursued it in the past."

"If you're hesitant about being gone at Christmas,

maybe we can all go for it," Maggie suggests, but I'm already shaking my head. "And why not, I'd like to know?"

"Because I have other plans." I set my spoon down and look at each of them. This is what I came in here for today, after all. "I'm going to ask Anastasia to marry me."

"Really?" Maggie screeches, jumps on her toes, and wraps her arms around my neck to hug me. "Oh, this makes me so happy. I *really* like her."

"Me, too." My tone is dry as I smile at Keegan, who's already pouring celebratory shots of the Irish.

"You have to ask her father," Shawn reminds me. "You have to be thoughtful about this."

"Are you sure you're twenty-seven?" I ask him. Shawn's always sounded wiser than his years. It's probably why he's already so successful in his screenwriting career. "You sound like a grandfather."

"If Da hears that you asked her without talking to her father first, he'll come all the way over here to have words with you himself, and you know it."

"Aye," I say. "I already planned to talk to her family. But I wanted to talk to my own first."

"You know we like Anastasia," Maeve says before sniffing her glass of whiskey.

"No matter how much you all like her, it changes the dynamics between us. And I need to make sure that you not only *like* her but that you love her enough to welcome her into our family, wholly and without reservation. Because once I marry her, it's for the rest of my life."

"Well, I should be writing that down and putting it in a movie," Shawn says quietly.

"We want *you* to be happy, Kane," Keegan says. "You've always been the one to look out for the rest of us. It's high time you did something because it'll make *you* happy."

"I do plenty that makes me happy."

"Not as much as you should," Maggie says.

"So, you're all in favor of it, then?"

They nod, all smiling and watching me with eyes full of pride and congratulations.

"We should help you plan the proposal," Maggie says.

"I already have it planned."

"But it should be romantic," Maeve says.

"It's bloody romantic," I shoot back at her. "I'm a romantic man."

"He may be a lot of things, but I've never known Kane O'Callaghan to be romantic," Shawn says with a laugh. "So, you'd better tell us what you've planned, so we can tell you if it's romantic enough."

I glare at my brother but tell them about the exhibit and how I plan to execute the proposal.

"Well, I'll be damned," Keegan says in surprise. "Maybe you're a romantic, after all."

"This is a surprise," Sherri, Anastasia's mother, says the next afternoon. I asked if I could meet with not only Anastasia's parents but her siblings, as well.

"Thank you for meeting me on such short notice."

"You're always welcome here," Ed says as he slaps me on the shoulder and gestures for me to follow him to the living room, where Amelia, Wyatt, and Archer are already sitting.

Archer looks exhausted. Haunted, if truth be told. I don't think Anastasia has talked with him since the night he got drunk at the pub and passed out in my guest room.

Amelia smiles and stands to offer me a hug before we all sit, the five of them all watching me and waiting for me to talk.

"Would you like something to drink, dear?" Sherri asks.

"No, thank you. I asked you all here without Anastasia present because I'd like to talk with you about my relationship with her. And how I would like things to move along going forward."

"Isn't this something you should just talk to Daddy about?" Amelia asks with a sly smile.

I shake my head no. "Traditionally, yes, but in this case, I think speaking with her whole family is appropriate. Family is important to both Anastasia and me, and I know that she and I consider how our decisions will impact those we love."

I shift in my seat. "I'm completely in love with

Anastasia. It's impossible *not* to be, as far as I'm concerned. And I'd like to ask her to marry me."

"I have some concerns," Amelia says, surprising me. "Not about *you* as a person, but about the situation. You live on an island, and Stasia's made her home in Bellevue, where her business is. Would you ask her to give up her career so she can live with you?"

"That *is* a speed bump, but not one that we can't figure out. Anastasia will do as she pleases, as we all well know. I won't ask her to give up her career, no. She loves it as much as I love my job. We will figure out a way to make it work for both of us."

We spend the next hour speaking about plans and intentions. I didn't expect them to necessarily just smile and say, "go ahead!" but I also didn't consider that I'd be given the third degree.

But I should have. Because this family is thick as thieves, and they stick together. They stand up for each other, the way my family does.

"We like you very much," Sherri says with a kind smile. "And we enjoy your family, as well. I think it's lovely that you wanted to speak with all of us today."

"Be that as it may," Ed says thoughtfully, "if a man is considering my daughter for a wife, it needs to be about more than our families getting along well. I need to know that you're going to step up to the plate every day, Kane, not just on the easy days. There will be times when you're exhausted, frustrated, angry. Or perhaps one or both of you is sad. Troubled.

Marriage is about those days, too. And it's not always sexy."

"You're right." I rub my hand over my neck, trying to pull my thoughts together. "Anastasia deserves someone who always has her back, no matter the circumstances or the mood, and that's the truth of it, Mr. Montgomery. I know there will be times of struggle, but she'll never have a moment of doubt when it comes to my loyalty or fidelity. Or my love. I'll care for her until my dying breath. I love her, the good and the bad. She's funny and smart. Dedicated. Hardworking. She's also stubborn and moody when she doesn't feel well."

I smile. "I know this: her love and dedication to her family are admirable. I'm proud of her. I miss her when she's not by my side. She challenges me and gives me a fresh perspective on things. I've already had the same conversation with my family because marriage changes the dynamic in relationships."

"I take it they gave you the go-ahead?" Archer asks.

"Enthusiastically so. It's with a humble heart that I ask you for Anastasia's hand in marriage."

We all turn to Ed, waiting as he watches me thoughtfully, plucking on his lower lip as he ponders my question.

"Well," he says, "I guess there's just one thing left to say. Welcome to the family, Kane."

"I have to ask her, but thank you, sir. Thank you very much."

CHAPTER EIGHTEEN

~ANASTASIA~

"Oh, my God."

I'm staring into the box, suddenly speechless.

"Happy birthday, darling," Kane says. He kisses the top of my head.

"Kane, this is just too much."

"Nonsense." He reaches into the box and lifts the amazing sculpture we saw at the beach out of the cardboard and sets it on my countertop for me to admire. "I've never seen your eyes light up the way they did when you saw this piece."

"It's so lovely," I whisper and reach out to touch the girl's hair. I spin and wrap my arms tightly around Kane, my face buried against his chest. "Thank you, *so* much. You couldn't have given me anything more perfect than this."

"Well, we'll see about that," he murmurs but kisses

the top of my head again, and then he tips up my chin so he can look into my eyes. "I hope this birthday is one you'll never forget."

"How could I?" I pull back and turn to the sculpture, examining it more closely. "I'll always have this to remember. I wonder where I should put her. Maybe I should have some new lighting installed over in the corner and put her on a pedestal to show her off."

"There's no rush in deciding that," he says.

"That's true. I'll want it to be a place that I see all the time. Maybe the master bedroom would be better."

"I'm sure you'll find just the spot," he says and reaches for our jackets. "For now, we have more places to visit before the evening is over."

"I do like it when you're mysterious like this." I push my arms into my coat and reach for my handbag. "It reminds me of when we first met. You were ridiculously mysterious."

"Just private," he says with a wink and leads me out to his car. Before I can sit down, Kane reaches in and comes back with a dozen roses that he left sitting on the seat. "For the birthday girl."

"Oh, they're beautiful." I smell them, fussing over the beautiful red blooms, and get settled in the car. Kane takes off, merges onto the freeway, and before I know it, we're headed through Seattle to Tacoma. Kane parks at the museum and escorts me inside through a back door. "Are we supposed to be here after hours?"

He smirks and leads me to my favorite exhibit, the one that we originally met in.

"I can be in here whenever I like."

I can't reply. All I can do is stare in wonder at all of the lit candles and the table set up in the middle of the room where the benches once were. It's set for dinner for two, with more candles and beautiful stemware.

"Kane, are we having dinner here?"

"Aye." He leans in to kiss me softly. Thoroughly. "Dinner will be served in just a few moments. First, I wanted to tell you how much more this particular room has come to mean to me. It's where I first saw you, fiercely drawing on your sketchpad, your tongue clamped between your teeth, magnificent blue eyes shining as the image in your head took shape on the page."

"I've always loved this room," I admit softly, gazing at the glass shaped to resemble the water, and the marine life floating around it. "It *moves*, which might not make sense, but—"

"It makes perfect sense to me. This space represents home to me, so I wanted to celebrate a piece of your birthday here, with a good meal and conversation, where it all began for us."

"Kane O'Callaghan, you're a hopeless romantic." I can't help but grin foolishly as he holds out my chair for me, and then takes the one across from me.

"It seems I can be. I never was before."

We're served delicious salmon steaks with salads

and rice, the servers coming in and out of the room quickly and efficiently. Where they're coming *from*, I have no idea, as there was no sign of them when we arrived.

When I can't eat another bite, I lean back and sigh, patting my belly. "I'm so full. I could curl up and take a long nap."

"We'll save the sleeping for later."

Kane winks and stands, takes my hand, and kisses my knuckles.

"Let's keep going, shall we?"

I frown up at him. "Keep going? Where?"

"I have a few more things to show you."

He leads me through the museum, explaining what he was thinking about when he made the glass for each room and what it represents. I've seen it all before, of course, but never like this. Not through *his* eyes. I have to say, it's absolutely fascinating.

"You should give private tours," I say when we've finished in the last room. "Seriously, people would pay a lot of money for this. It's so interesting."

"This is a private tour, just for you, darling."

He pulls me close and kisses me madly, and when he pulls back, I swear I see nervousness in his eyes.

"Kane? What's wrong?"

He shakes his head. "I've one more thing to show you."

He leads me around the corner and into a new space that I've never seen before.

"Oh, is this the new exhibit?"

"Aye." His voice is hushed. Reverent. He stands back while I walk through the room, soaking it all in.

It's a riot of color. Teal, pink, yellow, red, purple. The shapes are long and sinuous. If I had to describe it in one word, I'd use *sexy*. It's full of passion.

Suddenly, Kane's standing behind me, his hands on my shoulders.

"This room is different," he begins. "At first, I wanted to stick with just one color, but the more I thought and worked, I knew I could never narrow it down to just one. My feelings were too full of emotion, too raw, and it had to be expressed through color."

He runs his hands down my arms, then settles them once again on my shoulders. "When I began working on these pieces, I'd just discovered the full extent of my feelings for you. Realized that I was so completely in love with you, I ached with it. Just looking at you fills me with emotions the magnitude of which I've never felt before. Sometimes, it burns red-hot, like this." He points to a piece. "The times when I can't help but make love to you, claim you. And other times, it's a soft hum, like this yellow, when simply being with you fills me with joy and happiness."

I turn to watch him now, rather than looking at the glass.

"This exhibit is *you*, Anastasia. It's my dedication, my loyalty, and my love for everything you are. I can't imagine a day without you in it, or a time when you're not mine."

To my utter shock, Kane lowers to one knee and holds up a gorgeous diamond ring, the gem sparkling in the light.

"Please marry me, Anastasia Montgomery. Be mine for all time."

I fall to my knees before him and cradle his face in my hands.

"You're the best part of my life," I say, ignoring the tears falling down my cheeks. "Of course, I'll marry you."

He slips the ring on my finger, and then I'm caught up in him, his lips firmly on mine, kissing me as though his life depends on it.

"I'm going to make love to you, right here."

"No one can see us, right?" I giggle when his eyes narrow, and then he pulls out his phone and taps on the screen. "What did you just do?"

"Told the staff to go home, and I manually turned off the cameras."

"That's pretty good for someone who didn't know how to Google just a few months ago."

"I'm a man of many talents, darling." He slowly lowers me to a nearby bench. "Let me remind you."

Is this my life? Just a few short months ago, I was

admiring Kane O'Callaghan's work, longing to add a piece to my small art collection, and now I'm wearing his ring.

I'm engaged to Kane O'Callaghan!

And I'm running late.

I hurry into the restaurant in downtown Seattle that Amelia and I love to frequent, and glance around, looking for my sister.

She waves from a table in the back, and I hurry over, offer her a hug, and then sit across from her.

"Sorry I'm late."

"*I'm* sorry we have to celebrate your birthday late," she says. "I hope you had a good day yesterday."

"It might have been the best day of my life." I pick up my water glass with my left hand, hoping my sister will see—and admire—my engagement ring.

"Well, that's awesome. How's work going since you've been back at it? Are you all caught up?"

"Mostly." I do *not* want to talk about work. I want her to notice my ring. What the hell is wrong with her?"

"And how's your shoulder doing?"

"Just fine. It's pretty much back to normal now."

"I'm so glad."

We place our order with the waitress, and then I can't stand it anymore.

"Aren't you going to notice *this*?" I thrust my hand across the table and watch as Amelia starts to giggle.

"Of course, I noticed it as soon as you sat down." She takes my hand in hers and studies my rock. "Cushion cut. Probably three karats. It's absolutely gorgeous, Stasia."

"Thanks." I stare at it happily for a moment. "He asked me last night."

"And you clearly said yes."

"Clearly. You don't seem surprised."

"We knew it was coming. Not only did he ask Dad if it was okay, but he assembled the rest of us, too. It was really sweet. We interrogated him, but he answered all the questions right."

"Y'all conspired against me."

Lia laughs and then shrugs. "Yeah. We did. But it was worth it, right?"

"Definitely worth it." I stare at my ring again, still not used to seeing it on my finger.

"You have the biggest heart eyes when you look at that gorgeous ring."

"I mean, who wouldn't? And I seem to remember you doing the same thing when you got engaged. Holy shit! I'm engaged."

"We get to plan your wedding," Lia says, her eyes lighting up with excitement. "There are so many details to think about. When do you think you'll do it? Have you set a date?"

"He literally asked me roughly fifteen hours ago, so no, we haven't set a date yet." I tap my lips, thinking about it. "Maybe in the spring."

"As in, the spring coming up? That's like six months away."

"So?"

"So planning a wedding takes *time.* You'll need more than six months. Almost every venue is booked out farther than that."

"Maybe we can do it at Dom's vineyard," I suggest. "Or even at Kane's property. He has plenty of space, and it's really pretty out there."

"That's not a bad idea. If you do it later in the spring, the weather should be good."

We chat about what-ifs and could-bes, and before I know it, our lunch is over.

"I'm buying lunch," Lia says as she takes the check. "It's your birthday, *and* congratulations."

"Thanks."

"I'm so happy for you, Stasia. I like him a lot. Archer was excited for you, too, when we all conspired against you."

"You saw Archer?"

"Yeah."

"How is he? I haven't seen him since he got drunk and passed out at Kane's house a few weeks ago."

"He looks like shit," Lia says. "And when I asked him about it, he just grunted and said, if I remember correctly, '*doesn't fucking matter.*'"

"I'm worried about him."

"Yeah, well, when he gets like this, there's nothing we can do. He'll shake it off."

"I hope so."

~

"Do you guys *have* to do that while we're here?"

Kane's cornered me against Maggie's kitchen counter, kissing the hell out of me, but Keegan caught us.

"It's not like anyone's naked," I point out and laugh when Kane growls low in his throat.

"We need to be packing up," Keegan reminds us. "Not making out in the kitchen."

"We've packed five boxes," Kane says, pointing to the stack in the corner. "And I offered to have a moving company come in and do all of this for her, but she refused."

"She wants to clean and sort while she packs," I remind him. "It makes sense."

Maggie's house sold after being on the market for just a few days, and now she's going through the process of packing up and putting a good portion of her things in storage until she finds a permanent place to live. In the meantime, she'll be staying with Maeve.

Suddenly, we hear footsteps stomping down the stairs, and Maeve yells, "No, Mags. Don't do this."

We all turn in surprise when Maggie comes marching into the kitchen and goes toe-to-toe with me, her beautiful face red with rage.

"Did you know my husband?"

I blink at her, positive I didn't hear her correctly. "What?"

"Did. You. Know. My. Husband?"

"I met him that one time at the pub."

She shakes her head in frustration and paces away from me. "No. Before that. Did you know him before that day?"

"Maggie," Kane says with a hard voice. "What the hell are you going on about?"

"This." Maggie holds up papers she has clenched in her fist. "I found these up in Joey's office. They're receipts from *Anastasia's* store."

I take them from her and glance over them. "They're dated four years ago."

"So, answer the fucking question," Maggie demands.

"You'll not speak to her like that," Kane warns his sister before turning to me.

"I don't remember these," I say, frowning when I see that he ordered a cake to say *Happy Birthday, Shelly.* "Who's Shelly?"

"One of his sluts," Maggie grinds out. "Because it sure as hell wasn't for *me*, was it? And you *knew* her. Read the other one."

I turn to the other receipt and see a note in my handwriting.

Shell-

So happy for you, friend! You've found a good guy here. Happy birthday!

XO,

Stasia

I glance up at a photo of Maggie with a bearded Joey on the wall, and it all comes rushing back to me.

"Maggie, I know you're upset, but I'm telling you, I didn't remember this." I frown, thinking back to the night I met Joey in the pub. "You know, that night he came to the pub to pick you up, he looked at me funny. And I remember wondering if I should know him from somewhere, but I couldn't place it. And then he was horrible to you, and you left. I never thought of it again. But I do remember writing this note. Shelly was a friend of mine, but she moved away, to New York, I think, and we lost touch. I had *no idea* that the guy buying the cake for her was married. And he had a beard then, so I didn't recognize him at the pub. I'm telling you, I never put it together."

"I don't believe you," Maggie says.

"Well, believe me or not, it's the truth." I pass the receipts over to Kane, who takes a moment to read them over. "It was *four years ago*, Maggie."

She shakes her head, pacing the room.

"You *knew* her. You knew the bimbo he was sleeping with, and you didn't tell me."

"Maggie, she's explained it to you. There's no need to carry on like this." Maeve reaches out for her sister, but Maggie dodges her hand. "You're being unreasonable."

"I am not. It doesn't add up to me," Maggie says. "I don't understand how you *don't* remember. How, if you were so happy for your friend, you didn't recognize Joey when you saw him again at the pub. I think you *did* recognize him and you were covering for him!"

"Why in the world would I do that?"

"Enough," Kane says.

"Are you sure this is what you want?" Maggie rounds on Kane now, shocking all of us. "I mean, marriage isn't all it's cracked up to be. Don't do it, Kane, don't give up your biggest dreams for something that won't last forever."

"What in the hell is she talking about?" I demand, completely lost now and feeling blindsided. My stomach clenches when Kane closes his eyes, sighs, and then turns to me.

"She's completely wrong," he says, trying to assure me. "I'm not giving up any dream for you."

"That's not what you told us," Maggie says. "You said you're giving up the biggest exhibit of your career because of Anastasia."

I don't understand what's happening. Maggie's acting out, completely *not* herself, and now I'm finding out that my fiancé has kept something this important from me?

"Kane? What is she talking about?"

"It was bad timing," he says between clenched teeth. "And with everything else going on, I didn't have time to tell you. It's not a bleeding secret."

"So, he didn't tell you that he let something he's longed for most of his adult life slip through his fingers, all for you? Family doesn't hold each other back," Maggie says, shaking her head. "If you're worried that you can't have the relationship *and* your important career, this isn't right for you. *She* isn't right for you."

"You know what?" I hold up my hands in surrender, feeling angry and frustrated and *hurt.* "If this is how you act out when you're upset, I don't think I want any part of your family."

I turn to hurry out of the house, Kane on my heels. I need to get away. I need to catch my own damn breath. I'm breathing hard, and unless I get a handle on myself, I'm going to need my inhaler.

"Anastasia, stop."

I shake my head and rush to my car, but Kane reaches for my arm and turns me back to him.

"We'll talk about this. You'll not just run away."

I can't catch my breath. I have too many emotions rolling through me. "I don't understand what just happened in there, but none of it is okay. I need to think."

"You need to *listen.*"

"See? She's just ready to run at the first sign of a fight," Maggie calls from the porch.

"What the hell is wrong with you?" Keegan asks her.

"You go deal with your distraught sister," I suggest. "And don't worry about following me."

I jump in my car and zoom away, fighting tears, battling to pull in a breath of air.

I need my inhaler. But when I open my purse, it isn't there.

Because I used it at Kane's house this morning and forgot to put it back.

No problem. I open the glove box, but my spare isn't there either.

"What the fuck is happening?" I start the mental conversation I always have with myself when an asthma attack happens.

You're fine. You're breathing. You're going to be okay.

But the tears aren't helping matters, and finally, I have to pull over to the side of the road because I'm afraid I'm going to pass out. It feels like someone is sitting on my chest, and I can't get a full breath.

I try to talk myself through the techniques I've used all my life to calm myself down, but nothing helps, and that makes panic set in.

It's never been like this before, but I've always had an inhaler nearby. Instead of a grown man sitting on my chest, it feels like an elephant now, and it's getting worse. My vision is growing dark.

So, before I pass out, I do the only thing I can think of. I call 911.

CHAPTER NINETEEN

~KANE~

*A*nastasia peels away from the curb, and I turn to Maggie, absolutely ready to throw someone through a window.

"Get inside." I point to the house, my voice leaving no room for argument. "Now."

"Kane—"

"I said, now!"

Maggie whirls and marches inside. When the door is closed, and I'm sure I'll be putting my sister in her place in private, I round on her.

"You've no right to speak to *anyone* the way you just did, Mary Margaret."

"I've *every* right," she counters. "She met my husband before and didn't have the decency to say so right away. Why would she hide that?"

"Oh, for feck's sake, Mags," Keegan says, scowling.

"She explained exactly what she remembers—and doesn't remember for that matter."

"What, exactly, are you accusing her of?" I demand. "Do you think she and Joey had a fucking quickie right there in her shop?"

The very idea of it has my blood boiling.

"We don't know what they did," Maggie says, raising her chin. "After everything I've found out about him, anything's possible."

"You'll stop this insanity *right now*."

She frowns and looks down, then swallows hard.

"I can't believe the way you just behaved. Frankly, if I were in Anastasia's shoes, I wouldn't want any part of you either. Do you remember every customer you served a drink to four years ago?"

"Of course, not."

"I understand that you're grieving, and you're hurt. Every single thing that piece of shit did to you is *not* okay, and you don't have the luxury of taking it out on him because the fecker died. But Anastasia doesn't deserve the blame for that. She didn't do anything wrong. She didn't even know us when she made those cakes, and she certainly didn't know she was making something for a married man's mistress."

I rake my fingers through my hair. "If you simply don't like her, and you'd rather I not marry her, you shouldn't have lied to me the other day when you said it was all okay with you."

"I didn't lie," Maggie whispers and sags into a chair

in defeat. She looks exhausted, like all of the fight has gone right out of her. She's blinking, as if the person who just threw that tantrum is someone she doesn't know. "And you're right. She didn't deserve that. I just saw the receipts, that she signed them, and that damn *note,* and I was *so mad.* At him, for buying something thoughtful for someone else. And at her for not telling me that he'd been her customer."

"She didn't know," I say. "And now you've managed to not only offend her, but also insinuate that I've given up something very important because of her."

"I've screwed it all up."

"That's an understatement," Keegan says.

"I'll go find her and apologize," Maggie says, jumping out of the chair. "I'll go now."

My phone rings, and I immediately hope it's Anastasia, but Amelia's name is on my screen.

"Hello?"

"Kane, why is my sister *alone* on the side of the road having an asthma attack?"

"What?" I gesture for Keegan to give me the keys to his car. "Where the feck is she?"

"I'm not sure. She had to pull over because she was having an asthma attack and didn't have her inhaler. She called an ambulance, but—"

I hang up before she can continue and drive faster than I ever have toward the freeway. The only place Anastasia would have been headed is home. She can't be far.

I merge onto the freeway and make it only a few miles before I see her car and an ambulance behind it. She's just being loaded into the van when I come to a screeching halt behind them and jump out of the car, running toward them.

"Stop!" I run to them, my blood rushing through my ears. My God, I've never been so bloody scared in all my life.

Anastasia reaches for me, and I take her hand, then kiss it.

"We're taking her to Seattle General," the EMT says. "You can meet us there. We need to have her checked out."

"I'll be right behind you," I say, looking directly into Anastasia's scared blue eyes. "I promise."

She nods, and the doors are closed. I hurry back to the car and call Keegan's number as I follow behind the ambulance.

"What's going on?" he says immediately.

"They're taking her to Seattle General," I inform him. "She's awake, so that's a good sign."

"We'll meet you there."

He hangs up, and I toss my phone into the passenger seat as I drive behind the ambulance, keeping up with their speed all the way into the city. I park and run to the emergency entrance, but I'm blocked from going inside with Anastasia.

"You have to go through by the front desk," a nurse

calls out, pointing to my left. "Once we get her settled, they'll send you back to her room."

They don't give me a chance to respond. Left with no choice, I walk out to the waiting area and check in with the nurse.

"Please let me know as soon as I can go back with her. Her name is Anastasia Montgomery."

She doesn't even look up from her computer as she mutters, "Sure thing."

I'm frustrated and worried out of my mind as I pace the waiting area. I push my fingers through my hair and answer when my phone rings again.

"Sorry, Amelia, I should have called you back. We're at Seattle General."

"Is she okay?"

"She was awake and alert when I saw her, just before they loaded her into the ambulance. But they haven't let me back to see her since we arrived at the hospital."

"Awake and alert is the best-case scenario," Amelia assures me. "They'll get her oxygen levels stabilized and give her some breathing treatments and then let her go home."

"I need to have her car picked up."

"Wyatt's all over that," Lia says. "Don't worry about it. Let me know if you need anything, and please ask her to call me later."

"I will. Thanks, Amelia."

"There he is."

I turn, relieved when I see my siblings hurry toward me.

"How is she?" Maeve asks.

"I don't know. They haven't let me go back with her yet."

"I'm so sorry." Maggie's face is ashen and full of distress. "I'm so, so sorry. Kane, I didn't mean for this to happen."

"It's not your fault."

"Is there a Kane O'Callaghan out here?"

I whirl at my name and raise my hand. "That's me. Can I go back with her?"

"She's asking for you," the nurse confirms.

"We'll be here," Keegan assures me. "Give her our best."

"And please let me come back to apologize," Maggie adds.

I follow the petite nurse to the back of the ER, the same room Anastasia was in when she dislocated her shoulder.

"We have to stop meeting this way," she says with a weak smile as I walk in the door. She's holding a tube, and puts it up to her lips, breathing deeply in and out.

"You scared the bloody life out of me." I yank her against me, holding on tightly as my heart threatens to beat out of my chest. "I don't know that I've ever been that frightened, and you've given me a few scares in our short time together."

She doesn't say anything for a long moment, just

breathes in and out. Finally, when a machine beeps, she takes the tube away from her lips.

"This one scared me, too. If I'd had an inhaler with me, it wouldn't have escalated this far."

"Why didn't you have a bloody inhaler?"

"I used the one in my purse this morning and forgot it at your house. The weather's been bugging my lungs. And I don't know why I didn't have one in the glove box."

I pull mine out of my pocket so she can see it. Tears form in her eyes.

"Why didn't you tell me you'd given up one of your dreams for me?" she asks.

"Anastasia—"

"No, I need to know, because that's not who we are, Kane. We *support* each other's wishes and goals. I'm so damn proud of you. Hell, I've been proud of you since before I knew you. So why would you keep something like that from me?"

"I told you before, I didn't keep anything from you. At least, not on purpose." I kiss her fingers, relieved that she's sitting here, whole and well, and able to dress me down with her words. "The gallery owner from the beach owns another in Galway. He wanted to feature me in a show, but he wants exclusive pieces. By Christmas. It's impossible, Anastasia."

"Still, you should have told me."

"If I recall correctly, I was too busy with my nerves over asking you to marry me to think about telling you about the show. I turned it down, and that settled it. At least, for me."

"But you told your family," she says. "Which tells me that you asked them for guidance, or at least bounced the idea off them. That's what *I'm* for. As your partner. I'm not saying you shouldn't talk to them, I was just blindsided, and it was frankly embarrassing, especially with everything else that happened with Maggie. If the shoe was on the other foot—"

"I'd be angry," I finish for her as I press the palm of her hand to my cheek. "You're right, I would be angry, *mo ghrá*. It got lost in the shuffle of the past week's events, and that's the truth of it, but I apologize for forgetting to tell you about it."

"I hate the thought of you missing out on something that means so much to you."

"There will be other shows."

"But in Ireland?"

I shrug a shoulder. "I've been invited before, but it's usually Dublin, and while I love that city, I'd like my first Irish showing to be closer to home so it's easier for my grandparents to travel to it."

"I'm sure they would love that, too. Maybe you can talk to Trevor about a spring exhibit?"

"We'll work it out. Don't worry over it. Just breathe deeply so we can get you out of here and back home where you belong. My siblings are waiting out in the waiting room. Maggie'd like to come back to apologize."

"I know she's hurt," Anastasia whispers. Her lip trembles, and it breaks my heart. "And I know she's angry. But I don't think I'm ready for that conversation right now."

"I understand." Our heads turn to the doorway where Maggie's standing, her hands wringing at her waist. "But you don't have to say anything at all. I'll just say this and leave you be."

Maggie steps inside and bites her lip.

"I'm ashamed of myself," she says. "I was unkind, and I lashed out at you. You didn't deserve even one of the words that came out of my mouth today. I'm so sorry, Stasia. Truly and deeply sorry. I love you. I couldn't love you more if you were my sister by blood, and I hope you'll forgive me."

"Well, of course, I forgive you," Anastasia says, tears rolling down her cheek. "But you don't ever get to be a bitch like that to me again. Because I wouldn't intentionally deceive you, or hurt you. Ever."

"I know."

I stand and move away from the bed as Maggie hugs my fiancée, suddenly uncomfortable with all of the estrogen flowing through the room.

"I'll just go give the others a status update."

CHAPTER TWENTY

~ANASTASIA~

Three Months Later…

"Will you be making your own cake?" Alecia, my cousin Dominic's wife, asks me as she leads us out to the wedding pavilion at the vineyard. Kane and I came out today to have a look at the venue for the event we plan to have in just a couple of months.

Of course, I've been out here a few times in the past, but Kane's never seen it, and I want to make sure he likes it before we move forward.

"I don't think so," I reply as Kane slips his hand into mine. "I thought about it, but frankly, I want to just enjoy the day and not have to worry about anything as a vendor."

"I couldn't agree more," Alecia says with a decisive nod before turning to Kane. "Before coming out here to Cuppa de Vita to work with Dominic, I used to be a wedding and event planner in Seattle."

"She was the best in the Pacific Northwest," Dom says, flashing a proud smile. "But I stole her away, and now she handles all of the events out here."

"The Montgomery family has kept me in business for going on seven years now," Alecia says. "Jules found me way back when, and I've organized every major family function since then. Everything from weddings to baby showers to anniversary parties."

"So, it's fitting for you to take care of this for us, as well," Kane says. "And we appreciate you taking it on, especially on such short notice."

"It's not a problem. We had the weekend open on the calendar," Dominic says.

"Look at this pavilion," I say in excitement. "I can just picture all of the twinkle lights, and the Irish music. This is where we'll dance and have dinner. I thought that if the weather holds, we can have the ceremony over that way."

I point out to where Will and Meg had their ceremony, in the vineyard. Theirs was such a beautiful wedding.

"You can have whatever you like, darling. I've told you that."

"Yes, but I want to make sure you *like* it."

"If you're happy, I'm happy."

"Smart man," Dominic says with a laugh.

The guys hang back to talk about wines and grapes and who knows what else as Alecia and I walk ahead to one of the barns that's been converted to a ceremony space, should the weather not hold.

"I like him," Alecia says. "I know we don't know him well, but I see the way he looks at you. It's just the way all of the men in this family gaze at the women they love. I have to tell you, it's something to behold. He's completely over the moon in love with you."

"It's mutual," I assure her. "He's the best thing that's happened in my life in a long, long time."

"I'm happy for you. And I'm thrilled that you want to have your wedding out here. Have you decided on a honeymoon yet?"

I glance back at the man I love and smile as he catches me watching him, and tosses me a wink.

"Ireland." I turn back to Alecia. "We'll be spending several months in Ireland."

EPILOGUE

~ANASTASIA~

Six Months Later...

My muse hasn't shut up since the day we set foot in Ireland two months ago. The rolling green hills, violent waves, and temperamental cliffs of the landscape lure me out each day with a sketchpad in hand, along with my pencils and even some paints.

I fell in love with the Oregon coast when Kane took me there, and I still love it, but Ireland is in a league all its own. The people. The culture. Even the language is intoxicating, and when we return to the States in just a few weeks, I'll be sad to leave this new part of my soul behind.

Kane's spent hours on end in his uncle's barn, firing

and shaping glass for the show that Trevor Mullins has scheduled for just before we leave. Kane decided that he'd make the exclusive pieces right here. Art made not only by an Irish artist, but on Irish soil, as well.

The O'Callaghan family's inn is lovely and sits not far from the cliffs of the ocean. I've just walked down to what I've come to think of as *my* rock and set my pencil in motion over the paper when my phone rings. I glance at the screen and pick up immediately.

"Archer! I haven't talked to you in a while. How are you?"

"I'm fine," he says. In truth, I haven't talked to my brother since my wedding day. I miss my jovial, happy sibling. He's not been himself in months. I wish he'd tell me what's going on in that head of his. "I thought I'd touch base with you, check in, see how you are. Make sure married life is still agreeing with you."

"I'm wonderful. I love it here in Ireland, and all of Kane's family is super nice. You have to come sometime and spend a good chunk of time at the inn. You'd love it. But, enough about me, how are you? I miss you."

"I miss you, too. And your cake."

"You only love me for my cake."

"I mean, it's not a horrible reason to love you." He laughs, and it sounds so much like his normal self that it makes tears spring to my eyes. "I have news."

"Well, don't leave me in suspense. Gimme."

"I found her."

Elena.

I stare at the ocean, surprised. Is this why he's been so out of sorts? Over a woman he hasn't seen in almost two decades?

"Stasia?"

"I'm here. Does she know you've found her?"

"No. But she will, very soon."

The End

NEWSLETTER SIGN UP

I hope you enjoyed reading this story as mush as I enjoyed writing it! For upcoming book news, be sure to join my newsletter! I promise I will only send you news-filled mail, and none of the spam. You can sign up here:

https://mailchi.mp/kristenproby.com/newsletter-sign-up

ALSO BY KRISTEN PROBY

Other Books by Kristen Proby

The With Me In Seattle Series

Come Away With Me

Under The Mistletoe With Me

Fight With Me

Play With Me

Rock With Me

Safe With Me

Tied With Me

Breathe With Me

Forever With Me

Stay With Me

Indulge With Me

Love With Me

Dance With Me

Dream With Me

Coming in 2020:

Dream With Me

You Belong With Me

Imagine With Me

Shine With Me

Check out the full series here: https://www.kristenprobyauthor.com/with-me-in-seattle

The Big Sky Universe

Love Under the Big Sky

Loving Cara

Seducing Lauren

Falling for Jillian

Saving Grace

The Big Sky

Charming Hannah

Kissing Jenna

Waiting for Willa

Soaring With Fallon

Big Sky Royal

Enchanting Sebastian

Coming in 2020:

Enticing Liam

Taunting Callum

Check out the full Big Sky universe here: https://www.kristenprobyauthor.com/under-the-big-sky

Bayou Magic

Shadows

Coming in 2020:

Spells

Check out the full series here: https://www.kristenprobyauthor.com/bayou-magic

The Romancing Manhattan Series

All the Way

All it Takes

Coming in 2020

After All

Check out the full series here: https://www.kristenprobyauthor.com/romancing-manhattan

The Boudreaux Series

Easy Love

Easy Charm

Easy Melody

Easy Kisses

Easy Magic

Easy Fortune

Easy Nights

Check out the full series here: https://www.kristenprobyauthor.com/boudreaux

The Fusion Series

Listen to Me

Close to You

Blush for Me

The Beauty of Us

Savor You

Check out the full series here: https://www.kristenprobyauthor.com/fusion

From 1001 Dark Nights

Easy With You

Easy For Keeps

No Reservations

Tempting Brooke

Wonder With Me

Coming in 2020:

Shine With Me

Kristen Proby's Crossover Collection

Soaring with Fallon, A Big Sky Novel

Wicked Force: A Wicked Horse Vegas/Big Sky Novella
By Sawyer Bennett

All Stars Fall: A Seaside Pictures/Big Sky Novella
By Rachel Van Dyken

Hold On: A Play On/Big Sky Novella
By Samantha Young

Worth Fighting For: A Warrior Fight Club/Big Sky Novella
By Laura Kaye

Crazy Imperfect Love: A Dirty Dicks/Big Sky Novella
By K.L. Grayson

Nothing Without You: A Forever Yours/Big Sky Novella

ABOUT THE AUTHOR

Kristen Proby has published close to forty titles, many of which have hit the USA Today, New York Times and Wall Street Journal Bestsellers lists. She continues to self publish, best known for her With Me In Seattle and Boudreaux series, and is also proud to work with William Morrow, a division of HarperCollins, with the Fusion and Romancing Manhattan Series.

Kristen and her husband, John, make their home in her hometown of Whitefish, Montana with their two cats.

Printed in Great Britain
by Amazon